NO CHILD LEFT ALIVE

RANDY TURNER

 Drop Cap Publishing

This book is dedicated to those of you who are still in the teaching profession.
If you wish to remain in the profession,
you will probably not want to write this kind of book.

CHAPTER ONE

Using every bit of strength she had, Abigail Saucier tried to get out from under her boss. The sex hadn't been that great in the first place and when Bernard Feinberg fell asleep moments after its completion, the full weight of his 240-pound frame still parked directly on top of her, Abigail just sighed and accepted it as one of the penalties you have to pay if you want to get ahead in public education.

Somehow she even managed to fall asleep, but those blissful few moments of slumber were interrupted when Bernard began snoring, a methodical droning buzz saw that continued well into the night.

Thankfully, the snoring stopped at some point, though it seemed like it lasted for hours. It was then that Abigail noticed the blinking neon light from the bar across the street.

She tried to pry herself away, but she could not move. So the lights continued to blink and sleep remained elusive.

Now it was two in the morning and as Abigail tried to extricate herself from her fleshy prison, it suddenly occurred to her that Bernard not only had stopped snoring- but she could not hear him breathing.

"Bernard," she said quietly. There was no response.

"Bernard," she repeated, this time with a more insistent tone. Time stood still as Abigail tried in vain to hear even the slightest sound that would indicate that Bernard Feinberg, the superintendent of schools for the Franklin Heights Unified School District, was still among the living.

No sound, nothing.

That was all Abigail needed. The realization that her boss for the past eight months was no longer breathing seemed to give her almost superhuman strength. She gave one mighty shove and managed to move the corpse enough to enable her to slide out from beneath him. She took his pulse and found nothing.

Her first impulse was to call 9-1-1. She reached for the phone, but hesitated after dialing the 9. "I'm the assistant superintendent of the Franklin Heights Unified School District. I can't be found in a motel room with a dead superintendent. "Nothing I can do for him anyway," she said to herself, then went into the bathroom and took a shower. Bernard Feinberg had taught her a lot and had put her in a position to land a superintendent's job, but he still had the smell of a 63-year-old man who had let his body go to pot and Abigail could not stand to have that smell on her one second longer than necessary.

As the warm water rolled over her body, Abigail began to formulate a plan. First, she had to get out of the motel, and then she had to drive the 75 miles to the school. It was Thursday, so people would arrive at the school building at about 6 a.m. Since there would be little or no traffic, she should be able to get there by 4. That would give her two hours before the janitorial staff arrived.

She dried off, dressed, then took a cloth and started wiping off fingerprints from anything she might have touched. She carefully removed the condom from her former lover, wrapped it in a tissue, and placed it her purse. She could dispose of it later. Then another thought crossed her mind.

"DNA," she groaned. Though he was 63 years old, Bernard Feinberg had been an athlete in his youth and prided himself in his performance. He had received a healthy dose of Abigail's DNA at two different points during the previous evening. But no one had her DNA on file, she reasoned.

However, her fingerprints were.

All public school employees in the state were required to have their fingerprints taken. Abigail wiped down everything for a second time, leaving nothing to chance. She picked up her briefcase, took one last glance around the room, then left Bernard Feinberg's corpse and headed out into the night.

No one was in the parking lot. Abigail climbed into her car, which she had purposely parked in a far corner. She was grateful she had been forced to remain behind at school for a few hours for a meeting with members of the Franklin Heights Chamber of Commerce. Otherwise, she might have been with Bernard in the school district car.

As Abigail started the car, she was startled by the sound of Lee Greenwood singing God Bless the USA. She had neglected to put her cell phone on vibrate.

As she pulled out into the night, she took the call. "Mom, what is it?"

"Abigail, where are you?"

"I'm headed home. I didn't get out of the meetings until late. Why are you calling at this time of the night?"

"I couldn't sleep."

"It never occurred to you that I might be asleep?" Or under some naked 63-year-old man, she thought ruefully.

"I knew you would be awake," she answered and somehow she did. Abigail thought her mother could read her mind sometimes, a notion that made her shudder. "That deadbeat husband of yours never showed up. Your daughter is still with me."

"I am sorry, Mom. Would you mind taking Diandra to school? I am not going to be able to get home."

"You need to leave Bob, Abigail, and you know it. He is holding you back."

"Mom, we have talked about this before," and we will talk about it again, she thought. "I don't have the time to talk now."

"So you're too good to talk to your mother. You're just the assistant superintendent, young lady, not the superintendent."

"I know, Mom. I know. We have gone over this before."

"And we will go over it again. Don't use that tone of voice with me, young lady."

"I'm sorry, Mom. It has been a long evening and I need to go into the office early this morning."

"All right. I will take Diandra to school, but you need to do something about your husband."

"I will, Mom. I promise."

"And you need to be sending out your resume. You are ready to take over a school district."

"I know, Mom. I will."

"You are too good to be working under Bernard Feinberg."

"I know, Mom," Abigail said, wincing at her mother's choice of words.

"I love you, Abigail."

"I love you, too, Mom."

As she placed the phone on the seat beside her, Abigail thought, "I might get that superintendent's job sooner than you think, Mom."

It had been less than a half hour since she learned before anyone else that the Franklin Heights Unified School District would have an opening for a superintendent.

CHAPTER TWO

As she drove into the parking lot at the Franklin Heights Unified School District administration building, Abigail was tempted to claim the place reserved for the superintendent.

The temptation passed quickly and she pulled her car into the space beside it, the one marked specifically for Assistant Superintendent Abigail Saucier.

There was only one other vehicle in the parking lot, the beat up '68 Ford truck belonging to the janitor, whose name Abigail could not recall.

Hopefully, she thought, she would not run into him or anyone else. She had a lot to do and a short time in which to do it.

She used her key to enter the building, looked to both sides, then headed to her office, a much too small to her way of thinking room located directly beside the much larger office which until a few hours ago had belonged to Bernard Feinberg.

"Good morning, Mrs. Saucier."

Abigail jumped, but despite her shock, she immediately responded, "That is SAW-SEE-AY. It's French." Good Lord, Abigail, she thought after the outburst, you have to stay cool.

'Sorry, ma'am," the janitor said.

When I am in charge, Abigail thought, they will damn well know how to pronounce my name. As soon as the janitor went into a nearby room, Abigail inserted the key into her door.

"Damn!" she said, when it did not immediately work. She hated that door. Things would be so much better when she could move into the next office. After a few moments of jiggling the key, the door opened and Abigail zipped directly to the filing cabinet.

She quickly sifted through the folders of drudge work she had done for the late Bernard Feinberg until she reached a manila folder in the back of the top drawer. Written across the top of the folder, in all capital letters, was one word- "PLANS."

With these ideas, she thought, she could turn the Franklin Heights Unified School District into the model for public school reform for the United States. These plans could turn her school into a showplace of success, one that would be used to demonstrate to every school district in the United States the path toward accountability.

"With these plans," she thought, "no child will ever be left behind."

For too long, Abigail had listened to the excuses offered by teachers who insisted that standardized tests came straight from hell and did not truly reflect students' depth of knowledge. Those teachers simply did not want to put in the hard work necessary to succeed, she thought. When she took over the school district, she resolved, accountability would be the watchword.

Now thanks to one lucky break, she might have the opportunity to put her plans into action. Abigail withdrew the thick folder from the drawer, took it to her desk, and switched on her computer. She had approximately three hours until the normal work day began. In that time, she would solidify those plans and have them where they would dazzle the board of education and put her squarely in the driver's seat.

**

A maid discovered Bernard Feinberg's body later that morning. The police were called in, but there was never any thought of foul play or anything suspicious about his death.

He was in his sixties, he was overweight, his wife confirmed that he had a history of heart problems as well as sleeping in the nude- he died of natural causes. Nothing had been left in the motel room to indicate that Abigail Saucier had ever been there. No one remembered anyone else being in the room and no one had been seen in the parking lot.

The bar across the street had a video surveillance camera that would have picked up Abigail's furtive movements in the time right after Feinberg's death, but no one bothered to look. Not that it would have mattered if they had- the camera had been broken for months and remained in place to make people think they were being watched.

Word was received at the Franklin Heights administration building late that morning. Donald Duckett, one of the three assistant superintendents, took the call from the police, who took care of the matter so Mrs. Feinberg would not have to do it.

"This is awful," Duckett said as he broke the news to his fellow assistant superintendents, Stanley Kramer and Abigail Saucier. "He was such a wonderful man."

"You should know," Abigail thought, "You've been kissing his ass for years." Ass kissing to Abigail was a far worse crime than any involving things she had kissed.

"Shouldn't we come up with some kind of plan to reassure the district patrons and the board that everything will continue to run as smoothly as before," she said, quickly adding, "just the way Dr. Feinberg would have wanted it?"

"I don't think we need to be in any hurry," Kramer said. "We just found out he was dead. I would be surprised if things spiraled out of control."

"When I get to be superintendent," Abigail thought, Stanley Kramer will learn who is boss. Under the system devised by the Board of Education and Bernard Feinberg, Abigail was in charge of curriculum and professional development for faculty, while Kramer ran personnel and instruction, and Donald Duckett was in charge of buildings and grounds. The system was rife with tension for Abigail since there were times when there was no clear delineation between her duties and Kramer's.

As the three discussed the situation calmly and took care of the basics, including the announcement that would have to be made through the media about the superintendent's death, an unanswered question lingered.

Who would take charge as interim superintendent while the Board of Education made its decision on a permanent replacement? Since it was already mid-April, the board could hire someone to begin July 1, the start of the next fiscal year, but someone had to take charge for the next two and a half months.

She would have to be that someone, Abigail knew, since she was the only one of the three who had been a superintendent before, even though it was with a much smaller school district.

"You're the one who is going to have to take charge, Don," Kramer said, much to Abigail's surprise.

"Why me?" he asked. "I don't want to be the superintendent. I'm only a few years away from retirement. I don't need the hassle."

And that's why he's recommending you, Abigail thought. Stanley Kramer is a bastard. If Donald Duckett were interim superintendent, making the decisions that would have to be made, that would give Kramer the perfect chance to shoot for the job on a permanent basis.

"You've been with this school district longer than Abigail or me," Kramer said, though Duckett had only been there two months longer than he had.

"Does that work for you, Abigail?" Kramer asked.

"Of course," she said without hesitation. "Donald's the perfect choice."

Her fingers gripped the manila folder tightly. Somehow, she thought, she had to get to the board of education and let it know about her plans. She was not going to let Stanley Kramer or any man stand in the way of her getting this job.

If the Lord didn't want her to be superintendent, she thought, He wouldn't have killed Bernard Feinberg. And He certainly wouldn't have made her go through all of the trouble of being stuck under the fat slob for nearly six hours.

CHAPTER THREE

Why me? Walter Tollivar thought as he entered the Franklin Heights High School conference room for the first meeting of Abigail Saucier's brainchild, the STAR (Steering Toward an Achievement Renaissance) team.

The teams had been installed in both of the district's middle schools, all eight elementary schools, and the high school, with all of the smaller groups meeting as one district-wide team. The principal for each school had selected eight representatives, though even the principals had no idea what the teams were supposed to do.

Tollivar examined the motley group of teachers who were standing around the room swapping small talk, mostly about misbehaving children, small-minded administrators, and the untimely death of Bernard Feinberg. He did not join any of the groups. He preferred to sit and listen, capturing bits and pieces of various conversations.

As he listened to one conversation dealing with the candidates to be Dr. Feinberg's successor, he felt a soft hand on his shoulder.

"Are you all right, Walt?"

He nodded.

"Are you sure?"

"Once things get started, I won't have any problems," he said, standing and motioning for the newcomer to take a seat. Kayla Newman was a second year literature teacher, and a surprising choice by Principal Robert Stevenson for the STAR team, but a welcome choice as far as Tollivar was concerned.

It was only six years earlier that Kayla had been one of the students in Tollivar's third hour creative writing class, one of the few attentive students in the class, as he recalled.

At that time, she had been a mousy brunette, with thick wire-rimmed glasses, and a slight acne problem. That shy child was just a memory.

The Kayla Newman who sat beside Tollivar now wore contact lenses, had her hair cut in a stylishly short fashion, with blond streaks running through it.

During Kayla's first year as a teacher, Tollivar had been assigned to be her mentor and had spent many an hour helping her through the trying times that face all first year teachers. Like all teachers, she had gone through the doubts of wondering whether she was cut out to be in a classroom. There were days, sometimes due to weather changes, sometimes due to a forgotten dose of Ritalin that she had been unable to maintain classroom discipline, the bane of all first year teachers.

Still, as that first year progressed, there were times when Tollivar felt more like the rookie with Kayla playing the role as mentor.

As he looked at her, he still saw the concern etched on her face. "I promise everything will be all right."

"Are you sure?"

When Kayla took his hand, Tollivar realized that he had been shaking. "I guess I'm not all right."

"Deep breaths," she said soothingly. "Just take deep breaths. Pretend that it's just the two of us."

Tollivar followed her advice, breathing deeply and trying to block everyone else out of his mind. The touch of her hand helped. He could feel himself relaxing. It was comforting to follow her suggestion and imagine it was just the two of them, though in the back of his mind Tollivar still had that picture of Kayla in that classroom of five years earlier.

The blissful state did not last for long. "Looks like fun," a booming baritone voice said. "Can anybody join in?" No one ever slept in Michael O'Leary's calculus class.

The mood broken, Tollivar's hand began shaking again.

"Did I interrupt something?" O'Leary asked.

"No, Mike. It's all right."

Looking at Tollivar's hand, O'Leary said, "You need to go to a doctor about your little problem, Walt. It's not going to go away on its own."

"Leave him alone," Kayla said, going into her protective mode.

"Sure, sure, all we need is another loony giving public schoolteachers a bad reputation."

"Michael…" This time it was Tollivar who took the younger teacher's hand.

"It's all right, Kayla. "

None of it bothered Michael O'Leary. "I'm hitting the refreshment table. Anybody want anything?"

Just to get this over, Tollivar thought. And please dear Lord, don't have any team building activities.

***

A few moments later, the eight members of the Franklin Heights High School STAR team had arrived, seven teachers and the principal. Each of the tables in the room had been designated for a school. Thankfully, Tollivar thought, the high school table was in a far corner near an exit.

The high school team consisted of Tollivar, Kayla, O'Leary, chemistry teacher Shannon Roberts, debate teacher Ronnie D'Angelo, Harv Logan, head basketball coach Leron Hundley, AP (advanced placement) English teacher Miranda Harwell and Principal Robert Stevenson.

Tollivar pulled a small notebook out of his briefcase and began jotting down description of the room, the people, and what he remembered from the bits and pieces of conversation he had overheard. It was nothing he really cared to remember, but the act of writing took his mind off where he was and what he was doing.

Every once in a while he responded curtly to a comment from one of the others at his table. They had all seen him when he was blocking out everything around him and, for the most part, they respected his space.

The double doors at the end of the room flew open and Tollivar wrote what he saw. "Either Abigail Saucier or the reincarnation of Margaret Hamilton just entered the room."

He couldn't be blamed for his confusion. Abigail was dressed in a black outfit that seemed to cry out for the pointed hat of the Wicked Witch of the West, at least to Tollivar, who had a jaded view of upper administration.

"She's going to get us and our little dog, too," Tollivar wrote.

"Welcome, everyone," Abigail said with a singsong voice that stayed with her long after the few years she spent as an elementary teacher. "Are we all ready to lead this school district into the future?"

Some of the leaders sounded as if they had worked themselves into a frenzy, primarily the representatives from the elementary schools. Tollivar detected a bit more reticence in the middle school and high school leaders.

After a moment of silence for the man she described as "our beloved Dr. Feinberg," Abigail Saucier spoke the words Tollivar had been dreading.

"I would like to start with a little team building activity to get us in the mood for the great things we are going to accomplish together."

Real professionals don't need to be treated like children to make them perform better, Tollivar thought. He caught a glimpse of Kayla. She was giving him a knowing smile. One of the things he most hated...and most loved...about Kayla Newman was her seeming ability to read his innermost thoughts.

"We are going to bake a cake," Abigail said.

"All right," an elementary teacher shouted, for no apparent reason, except perhaps for a love of cake that she had obviously indulged for years.

"If I wanted to bake a damned cake, I would have taken home ec in high school," Coach Hundley said.

"It won't be a real cake," Abigail said.

"Then why the hell should we bake it?" the coach said under his breath.

Unfortunately, Abigail's super hearing picked up even that loud whisper. "What was that, Coach?"

"I said, 'Why the hell don't we bake the best cake Franklin Heights has ever seen?' Damn, I love cake."

"That's the attitude, Coach," and she began giving the group its instructions. The cake would have all of the ingredients it would take to make a great school district.

"We can bake it, but I ain't gonna eat it," Coach Hundley said.

"It's a metaphorical cake, Coach."

"When you start working on angel food, give me a call."

For a brief moment, it appeared the assistant superintendent was going to lose her cool, but her composure returned. "You have 10 minutes to come up with your recipe and then we will share them."

As the conversation began at the high school table, the principal took charge. "I assume what the good doctor means is that each recipe has the basic ingredients- we have to have excellent teachers, strong administration, communication with parents, and a dedication to learning.

"After that, each school has its own special ingredient, the things that it brings to the table that makes it unique."

The same kind of originality and uniqueness that Abigail Saucier would love to wipe from the books, Tollivar thought.

"Who the hell is this good doctor?" the coach said. "The only one I heard talking was that bitch in front."

"That's why I put Leron on the team," the principal said.

At least from Leron Hundley, Tollivar thought, "we get the truth."

***

After the team building activity, Abigail explained how the STAR Team would work. "The first thing we have to do," she said, "it to come up with norms, the rules we will follow whenever we meet. The most important thing is that we come to a consensus on everything as a group. Nothing is worse than a group where one or two people make all of the decisions. To function as an effective team, we must rule by consensus. Does everyone understand that?"

Does she think we're kindergarteners? Tollivar glanced at his watch. A three hour meeting and there was still two hours and 20 minutes to go.

"If you understand that" Abigail continued, "raise your right hand."

I'm not raising my right hand, Tollivar thought, sitting on it just in case his reflexes betrayed his better judgment, or in case he was tempted to raise his hand with the middle finger outstretched.

Out of the 90 people in the room, perhaps 50 raised their hands, all from the elementary side of the room. Abigail smiled. "Excellent, we have consensus. Now let's begin turning this school district around." She quickly added, "Just as our dear, beloved Dr. Feinberg would have wanted it."

Tollivar shook his head. "She has taken leave of her consensus."

"Damn," Coach Hundley said, slapping his hand against the table. "I wish I would have thought of that."

CHAPTER FOUR

It came as no surprise to Abigail Saucier that she was one of the finalists to replace Bernard Feinberg as superintendent. This was the reason she had come to Franklin Heights. She, unlike the other two assistant superintendents in the system, had previous experience as a superintendent, albeit in a much smaller school district.

She left that position when her husband had taken a job in Franklin Heights. She swore it would be the last time she would let Bob Saucier make decisions that sidetracked her career.

A screening committee consisting of board members, teachers, former administrators, and community members had narrowed the initial list of 37 applicants to three, and all three were scheduled to be interviewed, one after the other, by the Board of Education.

The first interview was taking place. Abigail was not impressed with either of her competitors.

Her fellow assistant superintendent, Stanley Kramer, was being interviewed. "They will never choose him," Abigail thought. "The search committee just picked him out of loyalty for all of the years he has been in the system."

The other candidate, who would be interviewed after Abigail, was the wild card. Carlton Dunn, as Abigail had once been, was the superintendent of a small school district. As far as she could determine, he had done nothing to distinguish himself and he was only 31 years old, not seasoned enough to lead a larger school district. A Google search on Dunn had turned up little. Apparently, the Sweetwater Unified School District had no online community newspaper, and no gossipy message board. Carlton Dunn was a blank slate. And education was far too important to put in the hands of an unknown nobody.

Abigail felt the vibration of her cell phone and quickly stepped out into the corridor. It would not look good to be seen talking on the cell phone as she waited for her interview.

"Mom, I can't talk now."

"Have you been interviewed?"

"I'm still waiting."

"You are going to get this job."

"I know, Mom, I know."

"Are you still coming for dinner tonight?"

"Yes, Mom. I have another call coming in, Mom."

After the conversation ended, she hit the button, putting her husband, Bob, on the line.

"I won't be home tonight, Abby."

"Big surprise, out with the boys?"

"Works for me," he said.

It was their longest conversation in months.

Abigail returned to the reception area just as Stanley Kramer's interview was ending. As she waited to be summoned, Abigail saw her other competitor enter the area. "Thirty-one," she thought, "he looks like he should still be in high school."

A secretary ushered Abigail into the boardroom. After a quick round of hellos and handshakes, the board president, Craig Martens, motioned for her to sit down.

"Tell us why you would be the perfect superintendent for the Franklin Heights Unified School District," Martens said.

With that prompting, Abigail stood, and began working the room. She started with an explanation of the ideas she had to revitalize the district, beginning with her STAR leadership team.

"With this team" she said, "the direction for this school district will be formulated by consensus, and I can provide the leadership to guide that consensus in the right direction."

After the leadership team, she talked about other initiatives she wanted to implement, listing them one after the other, as the board members attentively listened:

By the time her monologue ended some 15 minutes later, the board had learned of methods that would drastically increase scores on state standardized tests through a series of practice standardized tests and a required course in test taking, professional learning communities that would bring the spirit of collaboration to Franklin Heights, aligning teaching methods so students in all of the schools would be learning exactly the same thing and not be the mercy of the whims of renegade teachers, and the addition of veteran instructional coaches for every school, who could bring the benefits of their wisdom to young, inexperienced teachers (and also serve as an information pipeline to her, which she neglected to tell the board).

As she sat down, Martens said, "That was impressive, Abby."

Murmurs of agreement coursed through the room.

"Do you have any questions?" she asked.

Martens looked around at the other five board members, none of whom had anything to say. "No, you have told us exactly what we wanted to hear. Now we do have a few questions for you."

"Of course."

"One of the biggest problems this school district has been facing has been our high school dropout rate. Thirty percent of our students are not receiving diplomas and it has damaged us every time the state accreditation team visits our campus. And plus, of course, it means we have many young people who are starting off life with two strikes against them.

"If we were to hire you as superintendent, what would be the first thing you would do to improve our graduation statistics?"

"We have to stress the importance of graduation at a young age," Abigail said. "From the time our children are in elementary school, they need to know how important it is for them to graduate. We need to hammer home the statistics that show how much money they lose by not graduating and how much it increases the chances that they will wind up in prison.

"We have to let them know that their life spans could be shortened because they are unlikely to have the necessary health care if they do not graduate."

"That's all fine, Abby," one of the board members asked, "but what specifically would do you do to keep our kids in school?"

After an uncomfortable few minutes of hemming and hawing, advocating greater communication with parents and offering more classes during evening hours, she concluded her answer and the board moved on to other questions.

By the time the interview ended, Abigail was confident she had overcome the missteps following the graduation question.

When she left the room, she noticed the final candidate, Carlton Dunn, was combing his hair and straightening his tie. Perhaps he is a bit nervous, Abigail thought.

She crossed the room, extended her hand, and introduced herself. "Best of luck to you," she said, as the receptionist arrived to escort Dunn into the board room.

"Thank you."

He doesn't even shave, she thought. The 100 miles he drove for the interview would be worth it, though. Even an unsuccessful job interview is a valuable experience. Since Franklin Heights would have an opening for an assistant superintendent once she was hired for the top job, perhaps Carlton Dunn would make an excellent assistant. Dunn, she reasoned, would be someone she could control, and far less of a challenge than Stanley Kramer or Donald Duckett.

Her phone vibrated again. Since the interview was over, she answered it. "Diandra, I am busy, what is it?"

"I'm not going to be home for dinner, Mother."

"And why not?"

"Matt and I are going to the mall."

"Matt, you mean the young man with the tattoo?"

"I've been seeing him for six months now, but he has two tattoos. He has my name on his ass."

"I beg your pardon?"

"It's cute, Mother. He's mature for 20."

"You're 15. You're too young."

"You're just jealous 'cause no one ever put your name on his ass."

"You shouldn't talk like that."

"Don't wait up, Mother."

"I forbid you to go out with him."

"See you later, Mother. Don't worry. We'll use protection."

"Diandra!" But it was too late; Abigail's daughter was no longer on the phone.

"Children," she thought. She only had one, but there were times she thought that was one too many.

"Thank God I am in a job where I don't have to worry about children."

***

Carlton Dunn spent considerably less time telling the board a little about himself. It was only a couple of minutes into the interview when the board president asked him about the graduation rate.

"Interesting you should mention that," Dunn said. "During my three years at Sweetwater, our graduation rate has increased more than 20 percent and we are expecting it to go up again this year.

"There is nothing, I repeat nothing, that I take more seriously than making sure our children are given every opportunity to succeed in life and there is no way they can do that if they drop out.

We have to do everything we can to establish an atmosphere that will make these young people want to stay in school. If they become pregnant, let's have a day care center on campus so they can continue attending classes.

"If they have to work, let's make agreements with business partners so they can pick up a paycheck and not drop out."

The board members nodded as they listened. Martens said, "That's why we brought you in here for this interview. Dr. Dunn."

Dunn leaned back in his chair, a smile crossing his cherubic face.

"Could you work with three assistant superintendents, two of whom wanted the main job when Dr. Feinberg died?"

"I would consider it an honor to have the benefit of their experience," he said.

And so ended Abigail Saucier's chance of being hired as superintendent of the Franklin Heights Unified School District.

CHAPTER FIVE

The announcement that Carlton Dunn was the new superintendent of the Franklin Heights Unified School District was made during a press conference two days after the interviews.

The secretarial staff at the administration building suppressed chuckles as they heard the steady stream of obscenities and the sound of items being thrown against the wall in Abigail Saucier's office.

It was the first time they could ever remember "the dragon lady" losing control.

It was the newest girl, Becky, who had been working for the district only three months, who drew the unenviable task of telling Abigail Saucier when her new boss had entered the building.

"Mrs. Saucier," Becky said timidly.

"What the hell do you want?"

"He's here."

"Who's here?"

"Dr. Dunn."

For a brief moment, Abigail considered telling the school board to shove it. It wouldn't take long for her to find another job. She had paid her dues. "You are not going to have Abigail Saucier to kick around," But even as the words were forming in her mind, she had already put the notion out of her head. "I'm smarter than this pretty boy," she thought. "I can outlast him."

Her mother had said it best. "When someone gets in your way, run him over."

A flicker of a smile crossed Abigail's face. "Carlton Dunn will never know what hit him."

In the reception area, Dr. Dunn was talking to two board members and reporters from the area television stations and the local newspaper.

"These are the people who are the backbone of this school district," Dunn said, waving his hand around the room at his secretarial staff. "Whatever success I have here I will owe to them."

The platitudes continued for the next 10 minutes, until all of the questions had been asked.

Dunn did not notice Abigail moving up beside him. When he saw her, he said, "Ma'am, could you get me a soft drink?"

Abigail was tempted to say something, but she held her tongue. "Of course, Dr. Dunn. Is there anything in particular you would like?"

"Diet Coke if you have it."

"I will be right back."

"The son of a bitch doesn't remember me," she thought. "He can shove the Diet Coke up his ass. Or better yet, he can let me do it." Oh, how she would relish that. But it would have to wait for another time.

"Mrs. Saucier."

Her thoughts were interrupted by Dunn's words.

He continued, "I am so sorry. Becky here told me that you were not one of the secretarial staff. I have been so excited about this job that I forgot about meeting you yesterday."

"It's perfectly all right," she said with gritted teeth.

"Nonsense. Let Becky get the Diet Coke. Is there anything you would like?"

"No, I'm fine."

With the semi-apology out of the way, Dunn returned his attention to his interviewers. A television reporter asked, "What is the first thing you are going to do, Dr. Dunn?"

"Do you mean after I talk to you? Sorry, I couldn't resist."

"Damned jerk," Abigail thought.

"The first thing I am going to do is whatever it takes to improve the graduation rate for this school district. If I have to knock on doors and convince 17-year-old dropouts to come back to our high school, then that is exactly what I am going to do," Dunn said.

"Damned idiot," Abigail thought."

"I am going to meet with my administrators and let them know that from this point on our number one priority is making sure the teenagers in the Franklin Heights Unified School District leave here with their diplomas. We will no longer allow students to drop out."

"Damned fool," Abigail thought.

"We are going to make our high school the place students want to go to, not the place they want to escape from," Dunn said. "It is time that our high schools stopped being places where vandalism, crime, bullying, and anti-social behavior is the norm. We are going to turn Franklin Heights into the cool place to be. Am I right, Dr. Saucier?"

"Damned right," she said, her face reddening the moment she realized the words had escaped her lips. "Right," she added sheepishly.

"Any more questions, boys?" Dunn asked. "Thanks, fellas," he said as they began to exit.

"Have you got a few moments, Dr. Saucier?"

"Of course, Dr. Dunn. My time is yours."

"Come into my office."

It was not the first time Abigail had been in the superintendent's office. As she entered, she noticed the room was full of unpacked boxes on one side, obviously Dunn's belongings and already-crated materials from the Feinberg era. Bernard's wife, Delores, had his personal belongings removed earlier.

When had Dunn done this?

"I had my stuff moved in last night," he said, as if he had read her mind. "I am excited about this new position and the things I can do for Franklin Heights. And that's what I want to talk to you about."

"Anything I can do to help, sir?"

"Oh, please don't call me sir, Abigail."

"Carlton?"

"No, Dr. Dunn will be fine. I have always liked the sound of it."

"All right, Dr. Dunn."

"The board members tell me you are the one with the big ideas."

Then why the hell didn't they pick me instead of this overgrown adolescent, she thought.

"I am here for one reason and one reason alone," Dunn said. "I am going to increase the number of people who walk across the auditorium stage during our commencement ceremony.

"You are going to be responsible for everything else."

"Everything else, Dr. Dunn?"

"Everything else. Tell me about the things you would like to see happen at this school."

Maybe this isn't going to be so bad after all, she thought. "I want to make

Franklin Heights into a professional learning community," she said.

"Sounds good, tell me more."

As Abigail related her vision of what a professional learning community would look like, she noticed Dunn's eyes were wandering. He looked out the window. Every once in a while his eyes followed someone who was walking past the door.

Before Abigail finished, Dunn stood and said, "I've heard enough. Go for it and I will back you all the way."

"Go with the professional learning community?" she asked.

"With everything."

"But what about Dr. Duckett and Dr. Kramer, they will certainly have some ideas, too?"

"I'm sure they will, and they will need to go through you to get them done."

"Through me?"

"Absolutely. My plate is full. I am not going to have the time to do anything except my number one priority. Surely you can understand that?"

"Absolutely, Dr. Dunn. I will do everything I can to make sure you succeed with your plan to improve the graduation rate."

"Don't worry about that, Abigail. You do what you need to do. Stanley and Don can do anything I need for them to do. And one more thing- you can have the credit for any of these programs you set up."

"Do you mean that?"

"Absolutely, Abby. You don't mind if I call you Abby, do you. I had an Aunt Abby who was one of the sweetest people I ever knew. She made the best apple pie in Carstairs County."

"Of course you can call me Abby."

"Abby it is. We are going to make a great team, Abby."

If you say Abby one more time I am going to knock you on your freaking ass. Those are the words she wanted to say. The ones that escaped her lips were "Yes, we will."

"I need to get rid of this chair," Dunn said. "It has some weird stains on it."

Those stains should have put me in the superintendent's chair she thought. She eyed her new boss. He was not exactly her type. Maybe he would be more appealing when he started to shave. Still, she thought, it wouldn't take long. All it would take was proximity, leaning over his shoulder while they were working, "accidentally" blowing into his ear, surreptitiously placing her hand on his, again by accident, of course.

Carlton Dunn will be putty in my hands, she thought.

"You know, you even look like my Aunt Abby," he said.

And perhaps, Abigail thought, another plan of action might be required.

***

A steady rain was pouring in Franklin Heights, providing a serious challenge to the city's inadequate drainage system, as Tollivar pulled into a diagonal parking place in front of the First State Bank, unbuckling his seatbelt to preserve precious seconds.

The clock above the car radio said 5:28 p.m., indicating Tollivar had only two minutes before the bank would be closed for the day, except for the drive-through window, which stayed open another half hour.

Walter sprinted out of his Olds Cutlass Supreme, nearly forgetting to close the door in the process. As he reached the door, he saw the "Closed" sign. "No," he shouted, though there was no one to hear his words. "I still have two minutes."

Despite the insistent rain, Tollivar pulled his wallet out of his back pocket and checked his cash. Three dollars was not going to get it.

He looked at the drive-through line. There were only two cars. Surely he could make it that long. He climbed back into his car, started the engine, and began to back out, and then abruptly pulled back into the parking place, shut the motor off, and again opened his car door.

As he started to walk toward the drive-through, he saw three young men approaching from the opposite direction, wearing nothing to protect them from the driving rain. Tollivar remembered the three; all of them had been students at the high school the previous year, but dropped out less than two months into the fall semester, after spending most of the time on suspension for fighting, vandalism, and violations of the district's drug policy, and were widely rumored to be recruiting for a local gang.

For a brief second, Tollivar considered returning to his car, locking the doors, and heading for home as quickly as possible. He didn't need cash that badly.

"Hey, teacher," the one in the middle called out to Tollivar. "I remember you."

It would be hard to forget you, Tollivar thought, considering that the young man addressing him had pitch black hair, with blond streaks, a lightning bolt tattoo on his cheek, a large golden earring on his right ear and a small golden stud on his lower lip, while his forearms looked like an advertisement for Walden's Tattoo Shop.

"You are a teacher, aren't you?"

"Yes, I am. I have never had the privilege of having you in class though."

"Privilege, I like that. You guys like that?"

They let him know quickly that they liked it. Though both of his companions were taller and more rugged than he, it was obvious who the leader of the pack was.

"Wouldn't it be easier to go through the drive-through?"

"I like the exercise."

"It's raining."

His friends quickly agreed with that assessment.

"I would love to talk, fellows, but I need to take care of some banking."

"Well, Mister Tollivar- that is your name, isn't it?"

Tollivar nodded.

"It would be easy for three mean looking dudes to just jump all over you and steal every cent you have."

Tollivar did not like the way this conversation was going. "All you would get is three dollars and some assorted change."

The leader of the young hoodlums started laughing, which immediately trigged a similar action among his friends. "You thought we were going to take your money? Now that you mention it, it's not a bad idea." He scratched his head. "Naw, not this time. You'd better get into the line, Mister Tollivar. See you in school." When he saw Tollivar's face, he added, "Just kidding, little guy. You won't see us anywhere near school, unless it's after hours and we decided to take a computer or two.

"Just kidding."

The two cars had already gone through the line and had not been replaced by any others, so Tollivar ran to the window and cashed a check for $100. The girl at the window didn't think twice about him walking through the drive-through. It wasn't the first time Tollivar had done that.

"You know," she said, "you could use an ATM?"

"Maybe someday," he responded, carefully placing the five 20-dollar bills in his wallet and heading out from under the canopy into the rain.

The name of the young gang leader popped into his mind. "Rico Salazar." Thankfully, he thought, that was one young man he would never have to face in a classroom. There was something to be said for dropping out of high school.

***

"These are the obstacles we face," Carlton Dunn said, pointing at the broken storefront windows lining Harris Street in downtown Franklin Heights.

"And just why are we down here?" the school district's administrative aide, H. J. Hopper, asked his new boss.

"If we are going to improve the graduation rate, we can't afford to sit still. We have to go where the dropouts are and bring them back."

"These are vacant store buildings," Hopper said.

"Follow me."

Dunn, dressed in suit jacket and tie despite the surroundings and the sweltering 95-degree weather, walked into an alley, followed by Hopper.

"Make sure you get plenty of pictures."

"Of what?"

"We have to let the public know the steps we are willing to take to make sure no child is left behind."

Reluctantly, Hopper began taking pictures of the surroundings, capturing a particularly good one of a rat peeking around an overflowing garbage can.

"See the stairway at the back?" Dunn asked, pointing.

Hopper nodded.

"There is a rundown apartment up there, I have been told, and three 17-year-olds, all dropouts, live there."

"And you're going to talk them into coming back to high school?"

"That is exactly what I am going to do."

Dunn took the steps two at a time, while Hopper struggled to keep up. Too many years of double cheeseburgers and cigarettes had taken their toll on the administrative assistant.

"Get your camera ready," Dunn ordered, as he prepared to knock on the door.

Dunn knocked four times before anyone answered. A surly voice from inside growled, "What the hell do you want?'

Undisturbed, Dunn said, "I wish to speak to Rico Salazar."

"Rico, looks like a couple of queers are here to see you."

"I'm not a queer; I'm the superintendent of the Franklin Heights Unified

School District."

"Same difference."

Seconds later, Rico Salazar came to the door, his body, covered only by a towel, which was strategically placed over his genital area and not much else.

"If you're a queer, you should like this," Salazar said, smiling.

"I'm not a queer, I am..."

Salazar waved him off. "I know. I know. You're the superintendent of the Franklin Heights Unified School District."

"You seem to be an intelligent young man," Dunn said. "Why did you leave school?"

"Because I am an intelligent young man, Mister- what's your name?"

Dunn extended his hand, which Salazar ignored. "I'm Carlton Dunn."

"Well, Carlton, I would say you are done around here."

Salazar's friends chuckled at the pun.

Hopper glanced around the darkened room. "Is that a plasma TV?"

"You like? Bought it a couple of weeks ago. Had to get rid of the old one. I didn't like the picture." The expensive television was not the only sign that despite the impoverished surroundings Rico Salazar and his friends were not struggling to make ends meet. The room had new furniture, computers, and other electronic equipment.

Noticing the visitors looking around the room, Salazar said, "With all of this, do you really think I am going back to school?"

"You may be doing okay right now," Dunn said, "but statistics show that when you drop out of school, you are depriving yourself of thousands of dollars of income over a lifetime and you have a much greater chance of ending up in prison."

One of Salazar's friends took exception to the remark. "Are you saying I'm a criminal?"

"Oh, not at all," Dunn said. "I am just here to make sure that you don't go down that path."

"Sit down, Rock," Salazar said to his friend, pointing to the sofa. "The man is here to save us from being somebody's bitch. Don't give him a hard time. He never said we were criminals. Have a seat, Dunn. Tell your friend if he wants to leave here with that camera in one piece, he won't even think about using it." Hopper immediately put the camera into its bag.

"Mr. Dunn never said we were criminals, Rock. He wants to keep us from going bad. Care for some weed?"

"Beg pardon?"

"Just joking, Mr. Dunn. Now please, explain to us why we should go back to dear old Franklin Heights High and talk slowly. Chris and I won't have any problems understanding you, but Rock is a bit slow."

"Hey!"

For the next 20 minutes, Dunn cited one statistic after another in an effort to bolster his case for the three young men to return to school. When he was finished, he asked, "What do you think?"

Rock and Chris laughed.

Salazar said, "You talked me into it."

"What!" his two friends said in unison.

"Now boys, Mr. Dunn came all the way here, out of the kindness of his heart, to save us from prison and from being broke the rest of our lives. The least we can do is give school a try."

"I'm glad to hear it," Dunn said.

"I don't believe this," Hopper said, shaking his head.

Salazar raised his hand. "There is one little thing we are going to need, though."

"Name it!"

"If we are going to come back, you are going to have to pay us."

"Done!"

"I know your name, I'm just telling you, you want us, you are going to have to pay for us."

"And I am telling you, it's done, d-o-n-e."

"Are you sure about this, Dr. Dunn?" Hopper asked.

"Don't worry, Hopper. I will take care of the details later."

Salazar turned to Hopper "What are you waiting for? Get your camera out, Mister Cameraman. Take a picture of the new scholars at Franklin Heights High."

"Do what he says," Dunn said.

Seconds later, the three young men were posing as Hopper snapped one photo after another.

"Is that art teacher still there, Mr. Jarvis?" Chris asked.

"I don't know. Why?"

"He's the biggest superintendent at the high school."

Dunn clearly did not understand what Chris was saying.

"Jarvis isn't a superintendent," Salazar said. "He's just a regular queer."

CHAPTER SIX

August, at it always does, arrived far too soon for teachers who were just getting into the swing of their summer vacations. Though the school year did not start until the third week of the month, many teachers, including Walter Tollivar, arrived the moment the doors opened the first week of August to begin preparing their rooms. It was not part of their contracts; they were doing it on their own time, but most teachers were already hearing the call back to the classroom days before the fall semester began.

For Tollivar, most of the work involved preparing lesson plans. He was not one of those who settled on lesson plans early in his teaching career, and then doggedly stuck with the same plans- whether they worked or not- until he retired. He kept the plans that had worked, tinkering with them to improve them or to remove any flaws, and he tried new material and approaches, not only to reach his class, but also to keep him invested in the process.

During those first two weeks of August before students entered the classrooms, Tollivar liked to wander from classroom to classroom, talking to his fellow teachers, finding out what they had been up to over the vacation and spending time with them he would not likely have the opportunity to spend once school began. Many of Tollivar's fellow teachers were plastering their rooms with all kinds of educational and motivational posters, designed to enhance the learning atmosphere. Tollivar had never been one for bulletin boards and the like. He posted his classroom rules, a few guidelines for writing assignments, and then filled his bulletin boards with examples of sterling student work from past years.

He also spent time adding to the hundreds of books on the shelves that covered the entire east side of his room. Why he spent his own money on the books every summer when he only had a handful of students who even looked at them was a question he had never answered to himself in a satisfactory manner, but it was still something he felt compelled to do. He, like many of the other teachers, also spent money on paper and pencils for those recalcitrant students who never seemed to have either.

For Tollivar and most of the teachers at Franklin Heights the idea of a summer vacation was not exactly what the public thought of it. While the public, force fed nightmarish stories of teacher unions running amok and destroying public education by self-serving politicians, believed the teachers were taking it easy over the break, for most of the faculty members, nothing could be further from the truth.

Many were taking classes, some to improve their teaching, but most simply because pay scales are based on seniority and credit hours. For others, it was the vicious cycle of teaching summer school or taking an outside job just to pay back their student loans or to cover the costs of those college credits. Though the credit hours did increase salaries slightly, most of the teachers took them to build up the amount of money they would receive from their pensions on that inevitable day they retired.

For most of the teachers, the three-month vacation ended up being two weeks or less. And now even that time had passed.

Tollivar made his way into the high school auditorium for the back to school meeting the Franklin Heights Unified School District held for all employees on the first official contract day of the school year, two days before the students returned.

It was a glorified pep rally to Tollivar and he hated being shoehorned in with hundreds of district employees into an auditorium that barely held all of them. It was still 45 minutes before the meeting was scheduled to start, but Tollivar always made it a practice to arrive early and claim an aisle seat. It didn't help much, but he had learned to do anything he could to make things even slightly easier.

Large screens were on both sides of the auditorium to enable everyone to see the same thing they would be seeing on the stage. At least they didn't use instant replay, Tollivar thought, though he was sure that day would come in the not-too-distant future.

Every few minutes more teachers entered the auditorium and Tollivar could already feel the tightening in his chest and the trembling beginning in his arms and legs. He was still in his comfort zone, but he was already being tied up in knots because of what he knew was coming.

From the back entrance, he saw Kayla Newman enter and for a brief moment, he felt a glimmer of hope. But who was the man who entered with her? He was everything Tollivar was not- tall, young, good looking (with plenty of hair) and the two of them were laughing and enjoying each other's company. The one part of the meeting that Tollivar held out as his salvation was suddenly becoming just another part of a nightmarish day.

The two of them headed toward the area where Tollivar was seated, Kayla waving at him. Tollivar stood up and when she reached him, she threw her arms around him. "It seems like it has been a year, Walter. How was your summer?"

"No complaints," Tollivar said, wishing the words would come as easily to him in social situations as they did in front of 30 teenagers.

Kayla pulled away from Tollivar, far too soon to his liking, and took the arm of the man who had entered with her. "Walter, I want you to meet Tony Peterson. He is the new world history teacher and assistant basketball coach. We went to high school together here, but Tony says he never had your class. Tony, this is Walter Tollivar, the man who helped me survive my first two years here."

"Good to meet you, Mr. Tollivar."

"Walt."

Tollivar did not particularly enjoy watching Kayla and Tony Peterson talking and laughing, and that involuntary response bothered him. "My God!" he thought. "It hasn't been that long since she was in my class."

He tried to put the thoughts out of his head but he kept finding himself glancing at the two of them.

***

As the first official day for Franklin Heights faculty and staff finally arrived, Abigail Saucier had the same feelings she had when she was a schoolgirl. She was nervous, excited, and ready to get going.

School had always been a major part of her life. She could not remember a time when she had not been in a classroom in one way or another.

She keenly remembered the disappointment she felt when she turned five and learned that she could not immediately attend kindergarten. When her school days ended, she played school at home, setting up her own classroom, complete with doll students sitting in miniature chairs.

She vividly recalled the "good" students from those classes, Barbie and Strawberry Shortcake, and that nasty Ken, always stealing glances at the other girls when Barbie wasn't looking.

"Why am I thinking about that?" But the thoughts continued: becoming head cheerleader in junior high and holding on to that position through high school, taking the leadership role in Student Council and Future Business Leaders of America. But the business she had always been interested in was education.

She never had any doubt that someday she would be in front of a classroom- and she had no doubt that someday she would be the leader of a school district.

That day had come five years earlier when she had been hired as superintendent of the Rolling Hills School District. It was a dream come true, but the dream rapidly became a nightmare. She remembered the high school teachers who had opposed her innovative ideas for placing Rolling Hills on the map. How could they have been so shortsighted? Her plans would have worked if the faculty had only given them a fair shake. Now she was receiving a second chance. She did not have the title but she was going to be able to put her ideas into effect.

The auditorium at Franklin Heights High School was already nearly full when Abigail arrived for the opening day assembly. The assembly was actually a pep rally designed to get staff pumped for the upcoming school year. Banners were posted around the room for each of the district's elementary and middle schools, and the high school.

On each side of the auditorium was a giant television monitor, allowing those seated in the auditorium to look at what was going on right in front of their eyes.

After taking a quick glance, Abigail slipped into one of the rooms behind the stage where administrators were scheduled to meet before the assembly.

As she entered, she noted that a young woman was administering makeup to Carlton Dunn. He immediately spotted Abigail. "Abby, I was wondering if you were going to make it. Come here."

"Are you sure you are going to need makeup?"

"Abby, don't you realize that not only are we going to be on our district cable station, but the local media should be here. We have to look our best at all times."

"Of course we do."

"Looks like you could use a touchup yourself, Abby. When Becky is done, I can have her give you a once over."

Abigail gritted her teeth. "No, thank you, that will be all right. I will just step into the powder room before we go onstage."

"Suit yourself."

As Dunn continued to have his makeup administered, Abigail stepped over to the sumptuously laid out snack table. She took a longing look at the cream bagels, and then put a handful of grapes on a paper plate.

"Aw come on, Abby," her fellow assistant superintendent Stanley Kramer said, "live dangerously. You could use a few pounds."

The other assistant superintendent, Donald Duckett, joined in. "And don't you think that makeup could use a little touchup?"

"Look, you sons of bitches. You are not going to treat me like this. You were passed over, too."

"I didn't even apply for the job," Duckett said.

"Shut up. I may have to take it from Carlton Dunn, but I don't have to take it from you- and don't ever call me Abby!"

Kramer and Dunn chuckled, infuriating Abigail even more.

Dunn, a towel wrapped around his neck, stepped in. "Are we all ready for the pep rally?"

"You bet," Duckett said.

"Absolutely," Kramer echoed.

"Let's get the damned thing over with," Abigail wanted to say, but the words that escaped her lips were, "I'm ready."

"Great. How do I look?"

***

As the time for the "pep rally" neared, on the other side of the high school, a handful of students were enrolling, including Rico Salazar and his friends, Rock and Chris.

"Why the hell are we here?" Chris asked.

"I don't know," Rock answered.

"I wasn't asking you."

"We are here to be educated," Rico said, filling out the paperwork that had been handed to him by the registrar.

"I don't need no education," Rock said.

"I don't need any education," the registrar corrected.

"Then that makes two of us."

Rico laughed. "I've learned something already. I am going to enjoy watching you in English class. And to answer your question," he said, lowering his voice so the registrar could not hear, "there are more than two thousand students in this school."

"So?" Chris asked.

"That's a lot of people who might be interested in buying what we have to sell."

"Makes sense."

"Sure it makes sense."

Rock looked through the list of classes. "I don't see finger painting."

"For you," Rico said, "that would be an advanced class. Oh, man. Now that is a reason to come back to school." The three looked over the girl who had just entered the building. She wore a blue bikini top and a pair of matching short shorts that came to just inches below her pubic area.

"She's coming this way," Rock said.

Chris began to comb his hair.

"Too late, my man," Rico said, "she's already seen us."

She ignored Rock and Chris, stepped up to Rico and threw her arms around him. "We made the right decision to come back to school," Rico said.

"Mmm," the girl said, elongating her m's to show her pleasure. "You're going to be in school?"

"I have a thirst for education," Rico said.

"What's your name, gorgeous?" she asked, moving her body next to his.

"I am Rico Salazar."

"Mmm," she said, once again stretching the consonant. "Rico. I like that." She took her hand, pulled his head down slightly and gave him a long, slow, liquid kiss.

"That's enough for today," she said, pulling herself away from him, and darting off.

"No need to hurry," Rico said.

"I have places to go and you have to work to get into this cookie jar."

"What's your name?" he asked, as she neared the exit.
"Diandra. Diandra Saucier."

***

Once Tollivar found the Franklin Heights High School banner in the auditorium, he had staked out an aisle seat. Even that maneuver did not prevent the slight shaking of his hands or his increasing anxiety. He would have preferred simply reporting directly to his classroom or to a faculty meeting, anything other than the annual back-to-school pep rally.

His dread of the opening ceremonies had lessened slightly when Kayla Newman found her way to the seat beside him. "Are you ready to be inspired?" she asked.

"The best way to inspire me would be to scrap this assembly and send us back to the classroom."

"I know what you mean, but don't you have even the slightest curiosity to see what our new superintendent is like?"

"Not really. I have read enough about him in the papers and his face has been all over the TV news."

Not a seat was vacant when all of the Franklin Heights Unified School District employees were in the auditorium. The annual assembly, first started eight years earlier by Bernard Feinberg had become a tradition, with mandatory attendance required for everyone from top administration to the custodial crew and cafeteria workers.

The high school band, which always began practicing two weeks before the school year started, opened the ceremonies with two football pep songs, accompanied by the cheerleading squad performing a stunt and encouraging the staff to spell C-O-U-G-A-R-S. Sadly, two of the cheerleaders had letters transposed and proudly spelled C-U-O-G-A-R-S, much to the audience's amusement.

The ROTC unit presented the colors, with the High School Student Council president leading the audience in the Pledge of Allegiance.

***

As the Pledge was given, Abigail saw Carlton Dunn wipe a tear from his eye.

"With liberty and justice for all." Dunn turned to Abigail. "Don't you just love this great country of ours?'

Abigail nodded, but Dunn was already heading toward an area just behind the podium. When he got there, he asked, "Does anyone have a mirror?" An assistant high school principal handed him a mirror and Dunn checked to see if he needed to comb his hair. Though every hair appeared to be in place, he gave it a once over.

Dr. Stanley Kramer welcomed the staff back and introduced members of the Board of Education, who were greeted with polite applause.

Then a man in overalls stood from a front row seat and climbed onto the stage. "Is this here the Franklin Heights School?" the man asked.

"Yes, it is," Kramer answered.

"Well, I'm a fixin' to get me some education."

"Well, you have certainly come to the right place."

The audience was groaning since variations on this same skit had been played for the past four years. "If I go to this here school," the man said, "could I become a doctor or one of them there lawyers?"

"If you attend the Franklin Heights Unified School District," Kramer said, "you can become anything you want to be."

"That's what I was a wanting to hear. I was plumb scared to death I'd stay home from school and be an assistant superintendent." With that alleged punch line, the man removed his hat and false beard and revealed the face that the audience already knew was underneath- that of Assistant Superintendent Donald Duckett. Some laughed out of politeness, others laughed because they couldn't believe he was so willing to make a fool of himself year after year.

And there was more to come.

Moments later, Abigail emerged from backstage, wearing a white cowboy hat and having slipped on a pair of white boots.

"Is that the new school marm?" Duckett asked.

"Why, no," Kramer said. "It's Dr. Saucier and it looks she has a message for us? What is it, Abby?"

She glared at him, and then flashed her pearly whites toward the audience. "Dr. Kramer, I am here to round up the best staff in the state. Then we are going to corral our younguns and raise their scores on the SAP tests."

"You came to the right place."

"Are you all with me?" she shouted, but she received only a lukewarm response.

"I can't hear you. Are you all with me?"

Realizing that she might keep asking, the audience responded with a lusty "We're with you."

"Then let's get ready to go to the roundup."

After the opening "humorous sketch" was complete, the president of the board of education gave a two-minute welcome and told the staff how much he appreciated their contributions "everyone from the administration down to the janitors," he said, trying to include everyone, but instead just reinforcing the pecking order.

The next speaker was Franklin Heights's Teacher of the Year, high school debate instructor Ronnie D'Angelo. D'Angelo had a reputation of being one of the more charismatic teachers in the school system. He was in his late 20s and looked more like a movie star than a teacher, and in fact, he had played bit parts in three independent movies.

Since it was common knowledge that he had been in the movies, D'Angelo opened with a couple of humorous anecdotes about his brief acting career.

"Acting in those movies is a thrill I would not trade for anything," he said, "but that was not what I wanted to do with the rest of my life.

"Anyone can be an actor, but what you do and what I do every day is something special. We take children who come from broken homes, children who have experienced physical abuse, emotional abuse, sexual abuse, children who have lives so horrible you hate to think about it- but somehow, through hard work, through dedication, we are able to touch those children. We are able to make a difference in their lives."

After relating a couple of success stories involving his students, D'Angelo left to a standing ovation.

The lights in the auditorium dimmed and the theme from "Rocky," blasted from the speakers. The assistant high school principal announced, "Ladies and gentlemen, your new superintendent, Dr. Carlton Dunn."

As he stepped to the podium, the assistant superintendents, standing a few feet behind him, used hand signals to encourage the crowd to give Dunn a spontaneous standing ovation. About half of the audience followed the instructions.

"This is too much," Dunn said, as the audience clapped, though it wasn't that loud. Dr. Kramer motioned for more applause, and the audience went along with it.

"I can't tell you how excited I am to be in the Franklin Heights Unified School District," Dunn said. "We are the people who make miracles happen."

For the next 20 minutes, Dunn told the staff how the miracles would be even better with him in charge. "We are headed down a new path of enlightenment," he said. "And the most important thing we can do is to make sure we do everything in our power to keep these children in school."

That, Dunn said, would be the top priority during the school year. "The only way children can succeed in this day and age is if they stay in school and get that diploma. We are going to make sure that is exactly what they do."

And that starts, he added, at the elementary level. "On the first day of school, I am going to do something no other superintendent in this school district has ever done. I will personally go to every elementary school in this district and have my picture taken with each kindergartener.

"These children will know that if they work hard, study, and stay in school someday they can be just like me."

Dr. Kramer started the clapping, Dr. Duckett motioned for the audience to stand and everyone did, though no one knew exactly why.

CHAPTER SEVEN

"Get down!" Tollivar shouted to about a dozen teenagers huddled next to the east wall in his classroom. Most of them did as he said, squeezing themselves between the rows of desks. Tollivar made sure the classroom door was locked, and then he flipped the light switch, plunging the room into darkness. He was headed toward his students, when he heard a banging on the door.

"Mister Tollivar! Mister Tollivar!"

"It's Becky," one girl said.

"Shhh," Tollivar said in almost a stage whisper. "We have to be quiet."

The banging continued, "Mister Tollivar, let me in before they get me."

Without thinking, Tollivar unlocked the door, and pulled Becky into the room. As he did so, he noticed a Franklin Heights police officer shaking his head and making notations on his clipboard.

"I wasn't supposed to do that?"

The officer shook his head. "Every instinct tells you to open the door when you have a shooter in the hallways, but you can't do it. When you open that door, you're putting every one of your students in danger."

"But what about Becky or anyone else who happens to be in the hallway? Do we just sacrifice them?"

"Hopefully, we will be able to get in here and we'll take care of anyone in the halls. Your job is to lock down and keep your kids quiet."

Tollivar returned to his classroom. After all of his years as an educator, he still had a hard time keeping all of his duties straight during these emergency drills.

The drill ended a few moments later, and the students, volunteers who had agreed to come in a day early to help, were sent to the cafeteria for their pizza reward.

The day after the back-to-work pep rally in the high school auditorium- the last day before students would return to the classroom- was filled with meetings. During the morning, the principals reviewed safety procedures, announcing that monthly lockdown drills would be held to help students and staff to prepare for any possible intruders, or in the worst-case scenario, a shooter. The drills had become a staple in schools across the United States following the 1999 murders at Columbine and it had reached the point where practice drills were held to practice for the practice drills that would be held during the school year.

Franklin Heights would also have regular fire and tornado drills, at least one earthquake drill, and a reverse evacuation, in case a shooter should be on school grounds and students have to return to the building.

It was a far cry from the school Tollivar remembered when he began his teaching career 15 years earlier. Much of the morning sessions were spent reviewing new paperwork teachers had to fill out any time an accusation of bullying was made. Most of the extra paperwork would not prevent bullying, but would serve as insurance in case someone should decide to sue the school district.

After lunch, it was time for the session Tollivar had been dreading for weeks- the second meeting of the district's STAR team. The day's topic was "Building Consensus in our Schools."

The speaker once again was Abigail Saucier.

"That woman is too damned happy," Leron Hundley said, as he watched Abigail mingling with a group of teachers from one of the elementary schools.

"Nothing you can do about that," the calculus teacher, Michael O'Leary said. "She's being paid a lot more to be here than we are."

"In the old days," Leron said, "I would have sexually harassed her. In fact, I would have sexually harassed her all night. I would have wooed her and screwed her and…"

"That's probably about enough of that," Principal Robert Stevenson said.

"Didn't see you coming up behind me, boss."

"I kind of guessed that."

Abigail moved to the front, holding one finger in front of her face, a signal, which was supposed to be reciprocated by everyone else in the room, showing they knew it was time to settle down. It was a holdover from the days when she taught kindergarten.

Soon the room was wall-to-wall index fingers.

"Index finger, Leron."

"My mistake," the coach said, lowering his middle finger.

Tollivar could not bring himself to raise any fingers.

"This is not the way adults should be treated," he mumbled.

"Animals shouldn't have to put up with this," Leron said.

When the room was quiet, Abigail spoke. "As we form the professional learning communities at each of our schools, it is important that everyone buy into them, or they will not work. This is the first year we have set aside time in our schedule, before school every Thursday morning, to build our teams and make this school district the best in the state."

At that point, one of the elementary teachers shouted, "We're number one!"

"Oh, my God!" Tollivar mumbled.

"Take a look at the handouts on your tables," Abigail said. "This is what we will do to get this school year off on the right foot. For the first five weeks, during our Thursday morning sessions, we will learn the art of how to get the most out of our meetings. We will spend the entire hour each week in the 'forming' stage."

"We're having five weeks of meetings to learn how to hold meetings," Tollivar whispered to Kayla. She nodded.

"During these five weeks, we will work on team building..." Tollivar's involuntary groan stopped Abigail momentarily. Kayla patted Tollivar's hand. His dislike of teambuilders, those little games and activities that are supposed to bring adults together and turn them into a well-oiled machine, was legendary.

Abigail continued, "And we will work on building consensus. Today, what I am going to show you is how we can all work together, how we can all be on the same page, how we can all travel the highway to the same goal, and..." she took a long, deliberate pause... "we can eliminate disagreements and build a consensus.

"Now, I would like to start today's meeting with a little activity that will help us get to know each other a little better. I bet you would all like that, wouldn't you?"

Without waiting for an answer, she added, "I want you to start at the Madison Elementary table and number from one to six, then keep going clockwise until everyone has a number."

The principal leaned over to Leron and whispered, "I should have let you sexually harass her, Coach."

On that, the high school table was able to reach a consensus.

***

Karl Deuschendorfer, known to everyone simply as Officer Karl, was a familiar figure at Franklin Heights High School ever since the Board of Education had reached an agreement with the Franklin Heights Police Department to provide protection right after the Columbine shootings.

As resource officer, Officer Karl never had much to do. There was an occasional weapon, usually a pocketknife and one time an unloaded Civil War pistol that a misguided student brought for a history project. He broke up fights (the ones involving girls being the most difficult), lectured occasionally on the dangers of drugs, and always stood guard before and after school.

Seeing Officer Karl was nothing unusual for students as they returned for the first day of the new school year. Seeing three other officers with him was strange and the four men seemed to be on a mission as they headed into the building and walked up the stairs.

"Good morning, officers," Rico Salazar said, as the men passed him. Three of them didn't bother to acknowledge him. Officer Karl said, "You back again, Salazar?"

"Good to see you, too."

Salazar followed the officers as they headed down the corridor and stopped at the room of Teacher of the Year Ronnie D'Angelo.

"Get back, Salazar," Officer Karl said, as the other three went into the room. "We're not after you this time. And keep your friends with you," he said, referring to Chris and Rock, who were two steps behind their leader.

Salazar listened as one officer asked, "Are you Ronnie D'Angelo?"

"Yes."

"Mr. D'Angelo, you are under arrest for statutory rape. You have the right to remain silent, anything you say and do may be held against you. You have the right to an attorney."

Rock slapped Salazar on the shoulder. "They're arresting a teacher. I've waited for this to happen for years."

"Makes you glad you decided to return to school, huh? Statutory rape.

I never cared for D'Angelo, but I would never have suspected him."

A feminine voice from behind the three chimed in, "He liked to preach to the teachers that they should do everything they can to touch the children."

"You have to admire a man who practices what he preaches, Diandra."

"Oh, he believed in hands-on learning all right."

"Who is he supposed to have raped?"

"That would be my friend, Danielle," she said, a coy smile playing at the corner of her lips. "And believe me, it wasn't that good. At least that's what she told me. Of course, I would have no way of knowing." She brushed against Salazar as she passed him. "I bet you would be worth a girl's time."

    ***

The Franklin Heights Police Department called the school district's administrative office a few moments before arresting Ronnie D'Angelo.

"This is not the way I wanted my first year to start," Carlton Dunn said, wearing a path in the shag carpeting in front of his desk.

"What are you going to do, Dr. Dunn?" Kramer asked.

"I'm going to put Abby in charge of it," he said. "I have to get to Richardson Elementary, or I will never be able to have my picture taken with all of the kindergarteners today."

Abigail stepped into the office. "What's going on? You said it was an emergency."

Kramer filled her in as Dunn prepared to leave for his tour of the elementary schools. "Ronnie D'Angelo? But he was our Teacher of the Year. He was going to represent the Franklin Heights Unified School District all over the state. This is a nightmare."

"Dr. Dunn says you are in charge."

"Me?"

Kramer nodded.

"We need to issue a statement. We can't say anything about his guilt, but we can say that we will take whatever steps need to be taken to make sure nothing like this happens again."

Dunn stepped back in. "I forgot my cell phone," he said.

"Are you going to make a statement to the press?" Abigail asked.

"No, I am designating you as our official spokesman, make that spokeswoman. I will be doing some damage control."

"What do you have in mind?"

"I alerted the media that I was going to the elementary schools to have my picture taken with the kindergarten students. They all said it was a wonderful idea and they would send camera crews to Richardson."

"Don't you think they might change their plans since a teacher has been arrested?"

"Teachers get arrested all of the time," Dunn said. "How many times does a school allow every kindergartener to have his or her picture taken with the superintendent of the school district?"

"He's right," Kramer said, barely suppressing a smile. "It's a slam dunk for us."

As Dunn went back out the door, Abigail snapped her fingers. "Thank God we had never released the news that Ronnie was Teacher of the Year. Let's get us some positive press by naming a new one. Who finished in second place when the voting was done last spring?"

"I don't know," Kramer said.

"Me neither," Duckett added. "Wait, it was another high school teacher, wasn't it?"

"That's right. I remember. And this one won't cause us any problems at all. Stanley, take care of our official statement on Ronnie D'Angelo's arrest. I'm headed for the high school."

"But you're the one Dunn put in charge."

"And I am delegating authority."

"I guess that means we have a consensus," Duckett said, as she darted out the door.

It was the first time either of her fellow assistant superintendents had ever heard Abigail use the "F" word.

***

Abigail's cell phone vibrated as she climbed out of her car in the high school parking lot. "Mother, I don't have time."

"What are you going to do about this teacher being arrested?"

"What do you think I should do?" Abigail said, her exasperation growing.

"You have to take advantage of this. This could make Carlton Dunn look like an idiot."

"Any mirror would make Carlton Dunn look like an idiot. Don't worry, Mother. I have this under control."

"You'd better. Are you coming over for dinner tonight?"

"I'll let you know this afternoon. I've got to go."

***

"You have all written five paragraph essays ever since you were in middle school," Tollivar said, working his way around the classroom. "You have learned that you have to have a certain number of sentences in a paragraph or it is not a good paragraph."

A few bright and cheerful faces, mostly situated near the front of the room, were nodding and hanging on his words. In the back of the room, it was a mixture of students talking, texting, sleeping, and in one case, snoring.

It was the only the first day, but it was like school had been in session for weeks.

"A good paragraph," Tollivar continued, "does not have to have five sentences or six sentences. A good paragraph can have one word."

"Damn!"

"That was not the word I meant, Miss Saucier."

"She broke a nail, man, give her a break," one of her friends said.

"Sorry, I should have been more thoughtful." As he prepared to resume the lecture portion of his class, he was interrupted by a knock on the door.

He flipped on the SmartBoard projector and five sentences were displayed on the screen. "While I take care of whoever is at the door, if you would please proofread and correct these sentences, we will quickly learn how much," he paused, "or how little you know."

He walked over to the door, which was locked from the inside, one of the safety precautions required by the school district in case a shooter ever came on campus.

He saw the faces of his principal and Assistant Superintendent Abigail Saucier as he peered through the tiny window. He unlocked the door. "Yes?"

"Sorry about interrupting your class, Mister Tollivar," the principal said, "but Dr. Saucier has some news for you."

Tollivar didn't like the sound of this. "News?"

"Congratulations! You are the new Teacher of the Year for the Franklin Heights Unified School District!"

She made the announcement loud enough that all of the students in Tollivar's second hour class heard and a few started shouting words of encouragement. A voice from the back sounded a different tone. "How many students will he have to touch?"

Abigail glared at her daughter, did not answer the comment, and returned her attention to Tollivar, speaking in a lower tone so the students could not hear. "You can understand why we had to spring this on you suddenly."

"Of course."

"We have the papers you filled out last year."

"I never filled out any papers last year," Tollivar said.

"Of course, you did. Anyone who wants to be considered for Teacher of the Year has to fill out paperwork. You have to be able to tell us why you are a good teacher and why you would be an outstanding representative for the school district."

"I didn't fill out any paperwork."

"Well, no matter. You are the Teacher of the Year. We will let you get back to your class. If you could stop by my office after school today, I will tell you what your duties will be."

"Duties?"

"Oh, yes. Though it is an honor to be the Teacher of the Year, you are the man who is going to be the face of this school district."

A frown developed on the face of the school district.

"Well, we will talk later."

As she walked out the door, Abigail's phone vibrated again.

It was a text message.

"Bye, Mom."

Abigail turned in time to see Diandra smiling and waving.

The Teacher of the Year returned to his class and resumed what he knew was going to be the worst school year of his career.

CHAPTER EIGHT

"Mr. Salazar, would you please sit down," Kayla Newman requested in her most authoritative voice. It was hard enough to maintain discipline in a high school for any teacher, but when you only stood a couple of inches above five feet tall and looked more like a student than a teacher it was even more difficult.

And, as usual, her polite request brought no action from its subject. Whatever he was doing in the back of the room was clearly more important than poetry.

Kayla had a good idea exactly what was happening in the back of her classroom. She saw two crisp ten-dollar bills passing from Rory Stewart, a malcontent who was repeating her class after failing miserably the previous year, to Rico Salazar.

"Mr. Salazar, would you please sit down," she repeated, trying her best not to raise her voice. The last thing she wanted to do was provoke a confrontation with someone who did not have any qualms about selling drugs in the middle of a high school.

Again, Salazar did not move. "Mr. Salazar," Kayla said for the third time, "you need to be seated."

He slammed his fist against the desk, causing Kayla and several of her students to jump. "What is your problem, bitch?"

Kayla walked over to the wall, where a white buzzer connected her to the office. She pushed the button, but instead of an immediate answer, the only sound was a high-pitched whistle that always preceded a response from the office.

Salazar advanced toward Kayla. "You don't want to do that, lady," he said.

A disembodied voice called out, "Yes?"

"I need Officer Karl immediately. Please tell him to hurry."

"He'll be right there," the voice answered.

Salazar moved to within a couple of inches of his teacher, looked down at her and smiled. "You shouldn't have done that, Miss Newman," he said, the anger of a few seconds before seemingly vanished.

Rock, who was seated in the back of the room, started to stand, but Salazar waved for him to remain seated. "No problem," he said. "No problem."

Kayla made a move toward the door. She would have to unlock it in order for Officer Karl to enter the room. She looked at Salazar.

"I'm not going to stop you," he said. "Open the door."

Kayla didn't wait for the student to change his mind. She opened the door just as Officer Karl arrived. He did not wait for Kayla to tell him what was going on.

"I should have known it would be you." A few moments later, he was handcuffed and headed toward the principal's office.

"I shall return," he said.

She tried to retain her composure as Rico Salazar left. She did not know whether her troubles were over for the hour. Salazar's two friends, who had all of the same classes as Salazar, were still in the room.

No one said a word and Kayla was able to return to the examination of a Robert Browning poem.

She had the students take notes from the Smartboard as she typed up a referral form to e-mail to the principal.

***

Salazar was seated on a wooden bench outside of Principal Robert Stevenson's office, waiting for the principal to return from visiting a first-year teacher's classroom.

He slid his hand into his pocket and pulled out his cell phone and quickly texted a message. After he was certain the message had gone through, he replaced the phone in his pocket, put his hands behind his head and began whistling.

"Stop the whistling, Mr. Salazar," the secretary said. One of the things Salazar had learned during his previous stay at the high school was not to mess with Florence Pickett. She had been at the school long before he was born, and likely would be there long after he was gone. "Mr. Stevenson will be back in a few minutes."

"Yes, ma'am."

She was about to say something else when the phone rang. "Franklin Heights High School," she answered. "This is Mrs. Pickett."

Salazar listened as Florence Pickett said, "Yes, Dr. Dunn," three times in succession and then replaced the phone on the hook just as Robert Stevenson returned.

"Mr. Stevenson, before you do anything else, you need to call Dr. Dunn at the admin office."

Stevenson nodded, walked into his office and closed the door behind him. A few moments later, the intercom on Mrs. Pickett's desk buzzed. "Yes, Mr. Stevenson." She motioned for Salazar to go into the principal's office.

As soon as he stood, Salazar began whistling again, ignoring the glare from Mrs. Pickett.

"According to this referral," Stevenson said, looking at the screen as Salazar entered, "you called Miss Newman a bitch, you approached her in a threatening manner, and you very likely sold drugs in the classroom."

Salazar said nothing.

"You realize I could kick you out of school for that."

Salazar said nothing.

"It's your lucky day, Rico... I'm going to give you a second chance. But you will need to go to the in-school suspension room."

Salazar scratched his head. "You might want to rethink that."

Now it was Stevenson's turn to glare at Salazar. "You are not going back to class. I will not do that to any teacher, no matter what."

"Dr. Dunn won't be happy. And if Dr. Dunn's not happy, you're not going to be happy either. How about a deal? I'm not going to the ISS room, but I won't return to literature class either."

"And just where are you going to go?"

"It's a big school," and with no further words spoken he left the principal's office. Stevenson picked up his radio. "Officer Karl, get up here and follow Rico Salazar. I want to know everything he does."

Stevenson jotted down a note to talk with Kayla Newman, muttering, "This day can't get any worse." The intercom sounded. "Yes, Mrs. Pickett."

"Damon Marlowe from the Teachers Association is here."

"Send him in."

"Mr. Stevenson..."

"Yes?"

"He's not alone."

"So?"

"He's with Ronnie D'Angelo."

Stevenson was wrong. The day could get worse.

"And what can I do for you, Mister Marlowe?" Stevenson asked as the union rep entered.

"I'm disappointed, Bob. No small talk. It hasn't been that long since we were first-year teachers together at Packwood High."

"It seems like an eternity. Now I repeat what can I do for you?"

"I'm here to see what we need to do to get Ronnie reinstated."

"You have to be kidding. He is charged with statutory rape. He has to be put on a paid leave of absence until his case is settled in the courts."

"This is ridiculous," D'Angelo said. "I'm being framed. I never did anything to that girl."

"It's out of my hands, Ronnie. You know I can't put you back in the classroom. The parents would be all over me, and besides administration and the board are not going to let me do it."

"That girl is a nightmare. She lies as easily as the rest of us breathe."

"Ronnie, let me do the talking."

"You'd better listen to your rep, Ronnie," Stevenson said. "Besides, the girl who is accusing you of having sex with her does not have a reputation for lying."

"Not her."

The union rep put his hand on D'Angelo's shoulder. "Don't say anything else, Ronnie. Let me handle it."

Stevenson's curiosity was aroused. "Who are you talking about?"

"The one who has it in for me. Diandra Saucier."

"Is there anything you can do, Bob?"

"Probably not, but I'll see what I can find out."

"Thanks. We'll be leaving now, but I wanted to give you this before we took off." Marlowe reached into the breast pocket of his jacket and took out an envelope. "This is our official request for Ronnie D'Angelo's reinstatement." Marlowe smiled. "Consider yourself served."

***

Tollivar's heart sank as he saw Kayla Newman standing by her classroom door talking with Tony Peterson, the world history teacher. He was leaning in much too closely to her, Tollivar thought. And even worse, she didn't seem to mind.

"No, I can't be thinking like this," he told himself. It was only five years ago that she had been a shy, retiring student in the front row of his class, with a flair for nearly every kind of writing she tackled, everything from poetry to essays to short stories.

But the woman in front of him was not that shy, retiring high school senior.

And she just noticed him approaching.

"Walter, congratulations!"

"Congratulations," Peterson said. "What for?"

"You're looking at the new Franklin Heights Unified School District Teacher of the Year."

"All right. Good job, Tollivar."

"Thanks. Kayla, I never filled out any paperwork for that, did you…"

She was nodding before he finished the question. "You deserve this and I knew you would never even consider applying."

"I appreciate the thought, but I am not at all sure this is what I want."

"We need you, Walt. As much as everyone liked Ronnie D'Angelo, he was not the kind of person who could use this position to improve the school district."

"Kayla, I don't know what you have heard about Teacher of the Year, but generally, all that person does is go around talking to Rotary Clubs and the Chamber of Commerce and tell the business community what a great school district we have."

"That's the way it has been, Walt. That's not the way it has to be. You are a person who can make it into something much, much more." She put her hand on his. "You have always had the ability to inspire people, Walt, and not just high school students."

Tollivar had been set to turn down the position. There was nothing in the world that would have swayed him from that action.

Until now.

"I'll give it my best shot," he said.

***

"So how do these SCRUTINY tests work?" Abigail asked, as she examined the sales brochure the testing company salesman had given her.

"As you know, Doctor Saucier, our company, Brockton-McGill, is contracted to prepare the annual statewide standardized tests, the ones that make or break your school system."

"You certainly do not have to tell me that, Gary. Preparing our children to excel on the SAP tests is the most important thing we do at this school."

"Exactly and that's why you need SCRUTINY. During the course of the year, your students will take seven tests designed to help them on the SAP."

"And what guarantee do I have that these tests will work?"

"We're the ones who make the SAP tests. Who would be better able to help you get ready for them?"

"And how much would this cost the school district?"

"Since you would be one of the first districts to try SCRUTINY, we can start you as a pilot program. Instead of our normal $100,000 charge for a school with your enrollment, we would only charge you $50,000."

Abigail nodded her head slowly. "I like the sound of this, Gary. Can you give me a little time to think about it?"

"The option to be a pilot school is only open for 24 hours."

"I will get back to you first thing tomorrow morning."

"Excellent."

After the Brockton-McGill salesman left the office, Stanley Kramer asked, "Are you sure we can afford something like this?"

"We can't afford not to take it," Abigail said. "Our scores were down at the high school and at the middle schools last year. We have to do something."

"But this hasn't been proven."

"The same company makes the tests that makes the SAP tests, do you really think they would let us fail and damage future sales?"

"Hmm, you may have a point."

"And since they are not going to let us fail, we might as well take full advantage of it."

"What are you thinking, Abby?"

She glared at him, and then responded, "We're not only going to buy the SCRUTINY tests, we're going to arrange our entire curriculum around them."

"Shouldn't we check with Dr. Dunn before we commit to this?"

"He is too busy increasing our graduation rate. We'll call in the curriculum specialists for a meeting this afternoon and get the ball rolling.

"We're going to knock the top off the SAP tests."

***

"Thank you for taking time out of your busy schedule, Mr. Tollivar. I wanted to let you know a little bit more about your duties as Teacher of the Year."

Actually, Tolliver had not taken time out of his schedule. He had to cancel a meeting of the Writing Club and delay grading 150 essays. A more fitting description would have been command performance. "No problem, Dr. Saucier. I want to help this school district in any way I can."

She handed him a piece of paper, which contained a list of dates and places. "This is a preliminary list of your speaking engagements for the fall semester."

Nearly every week, beginning in October, was filled with Rotary Club luncheons. Elks Club dinners, Chamber of Commerce meetings, and events held by other clubs and organizations.

"Some of these are being held during school hours," he said. "In fact, most of these take place during school hours."

"That is true, Mr. Tollivar. That's when most of these groups meet. If we want to be able to reach these people and let them know the good things that are happening in the Franklin Heights Unified School District, we can't expect them to come to us. We have to go to them."

"I understand that, but how can I be the Teacher of the Year if I am not in my classroom teaching?"

"It's all a matter of keeping your priorities in order."

"But isn't teaching children my number one priority?"

"Oh, of course, absolutely, but nothing about your new duties is going to keep you from being able to do that."

"If I'm not in class?"

"We have an excellent corps of substitute teachers, as I am sure you are well aware."

"I haven't had a substitute in all of my years of teaching, Dr. Saucier. I take pride in being in the classroom every day."

"Be that as it may, in order for you to serve your school district, and of course, the children in this school district, you are going to have to step out of the classroom every once in a while. I am sure you will have excellent lesson plans prepared for the substitutes. You will notice that I do not have any speaking engagements arranged for September." She reached into her desk drawer and pulled out another stack of papers. "During the next few weeks, I would like you to study these talking points. These are the things we would like you to emphasize when you go out in front of the public."

As Tollivar examined the papers, he noticed they included not only a list of talking points, but entire speeches. Some emphasized preparation for the SAP tests; others talked about the district initiative to improve the graduation rate, while others talked about the value of the STAR leadership group and how it was designed to improve education throughout the school district.

"Pardon me for saying this, Dr. Saucier, but I thought you were interested in me providing some insight from my background as an educator."

"Oh, of course, of course, Mr. Tollivar. These are only some things to help you as you prepare your presentations. I knew you wouldn't have any trouble with these since these programs were all enacted through a consensus of our faculty and administration."

"I will look these over."

"Thank you, Mr. Tollivar. I must apologize to you, but I need to be at one of the elementary schools in a few minutes. If you could see yourself out."

Tollivar was shaking his head as he headed toward the door.

Seeing that, Abigail added, "Don't worry. You will do fine. Once you have spoken to a few of these groups, it will come naturally to you."

Speaking to the groups was not the problem, Tollivar thought. Being in the crowds at these meetings was going to be a nightmare.

***

As the head of the Franklin Heights Unified School District's technology department hunched over his computer, Carlton Dunn looked over his shoulder, peering intently at the screen.

"What do you think?" he asked.

"I like the profile shot."

Dunn nodded. "I do, too. Let's go with it."

"Are you absolutely sure you don't want to go with a picture of the high school or maybe a cougar. That is our school mascot. People are familiar with it."

"No, no," Dunn said, his voice ringing with certainty. "The people in this school district need to be reassured that I am in charge."

"I know I'm reassured," the tech chief said, though Dunn did not pick up on the trace of sarcasm in his voice.

"Good. That's the way everyone else will feel, too. Go ahead and put it on line."

"Are you sure?"

"Absolutely. It is high time that we spread the word online about all of the good things that are going on here."

"Well, start spreading the news. We're on Facebook."

Dunn admired the page. "I'll send out an e-mail to the staff. Everyone will 'like' us on Facebook and we will offer a bonus to the staff member who successfully invites the most people to our page. I will have our new public relations coordinator start typing up positive information to put on the page every day. Isn't it exciting?"

"Oh, yeah. No doubt about it. When did we get a public relations coor-dinator?"

"I hired her today. She was a steal for $80,000 a year."

"The taxpayers are lucky to have you in charge of their money."

"Of course they are and this way we can be sure that they know that. Now tell me one more thing- When you get our Twitter account set up, will we able to have my picture on it, too?"

CHAPTER NINE

OCTOBER

This is the place," Salazar said, looking at the number above the apartment door. "It don't look like anybody's home," Chris said. "He's here. I guarantee you. Knock on the door, Rock."

Rock pounded four times.

No answer.

"Do it again."

The second pounding brought no answer.

"Stay here, I'm going around to the back." Salazar worked his way around the small rundown rental house and saw that a window was open. He motioned to Chris. "We're going to give Lucas Brock a little surprise. "There's room enough to climb in."

"Are you sure?"

"Brock's a wimp. He's not going to do anything."

"Okay," Chris sounded hesitant.

"All right. I'll go in first." Salazar climbed through the window. No lights were on in the house. That was not the way it was when they came to the door. Salazar distinctly remembered seeing a light in what appeared to be a bedroom window.

"Keep quiet," he whispered, as Rock kept pounding the door outside.

"You don't think he's got a gun do you?"

"A kid like that? He's scared to death of his own shadow."

Salazar and Chris tiptoed through the hallway. Salazar heard a faint shuffling sound in one of the rooms. "Ready?"

Chris nodded.

Salazar started to reach for the doorknob, then thought better of it and kicked the door.

"Little Lucas?" he called out. "Little Lucas?"

The boy did not respond, but Salazar could hear breathing, punctuated by a sharp wheezing sound. "Come out from behind that bed, Little Lucas."

"Are you sure he's there, Rico?"

"Just wait."

Seconds later, the boy emerged, his hands held above his head.

Salazar laughed. "Put your hands down, Little Lucas. We're not going to shoot you."

"Then why are you here? I've seen what you do at school?"

"Why, Little Lucas, are you calling us bullies?"

"No, no. That's not what I meant."

"Oh, I am sure it isn't. Now we're all friends here and Chris and I are concerned about you." Rock pounded on the door again. "Rock, you can stop now!"

When the pounding ceased, Salazar turned again to Lucas, "We were worried about you."

"About me?"

"Of course, Little Lucas. Chris and I are caring people, aren't we, Chris?"

"Yeah, we care a lot."

"Little Lucas, you haven't been in school all week and we were worried about you."

"I haven't been feeling well."

"You look just fine to me, though it looks like you may have wet your pants."

The boy looked away, ashamed.

"You will be back in school tomorrow."

"No, I'm still sick," he protested.

"You aren't understanding me, Little Lucas. You will be back in school tomorrow- or we will be back tomorrow night. Do you understand what I am saying?"

The boy nodded, tears beginning to stream down his face.

"I believe Little Lucas has the message, Chris."

"Yeah, he's got the message."

Salazar and Chris left Lucas Brock crying on his bedroom floor.

"Dunn will like this," Salazar said. "Another success story in keeping the dropout rate down."

"Us keeping kids in school," Chris said. "Who would have ever thought?"

"It's the old spare the rod, spoil the child bit," Salazar said.

"What?"

"We're not going to let these little pussies drop out. Anybody tries to drop out is going to get the hell beat out of them."

"I don't know why no one has ever tried this before."

***

"How are your SCRUTINY tests going, Abby?"

"We are scheduled to take the second round of tests tomorrow, Dr. Dunn."

This was the first time the superintendent had shown any interest in the tests.

"Well, keep up the good work, Abby. I have to go see the Chamber of Commerce Board about the graduation task force.

So much for interest in the SCRUTINY tests. The lack of interest did not bother Abigail. The more Carlton Dunn stayed out of her way, the better she liked it.

Her cell phone vibrated. She checked the caller ID. "Bob. What the hell does he want? I know he won't be coming home tonight." Nor did she want him there. A husband was the major drawback of marriage for any woman.

"Honey, I won't be home tonight," Bob Saucier said.

"You didn't need to call."

"Just had to tell you I love you."

"I love you, too," she said, with a noticeable lack of passion.

After the call ended, she dialed the high school principal's cell.

"Bob, Abigail Saucier. We have lined up 25 substitute teachers for your classes tomorrow so you can have your teachers hear Mark Masters."

"Dr. Saucier, are you sure that we have to send so many teachers? We are giving your SCRUTINY tests tomorrow. You know how students behave when there are substitutes in the building."

"Then you need to make sure that you keep them in order. It is important that our teachers be exposed to Mr. Masters. When we went to his seminar in Dallas this summer, he presented some ideas that could revolutionize this school district."

"I won't be able to keep an eye on the substitutes, Dr. Saucier. You are requiring me to be at the seminar. "

"Make sure the vice principal is up to speed. He's a good man; I am sure he can handle it."

"I am sure he could too, Dr. Saucier, but you are also requiring him to be there."

"My god, Bob, you are a professional. Suck it up and get the job done. Since when does education stop just because 25 teachers and two administrators are out of the building for one day?"

Robert Stevenson sighed. "All right. We'll be there."

"One more thing. How are we doing with preparation for the SCRUTINY tests?"

"What do you mean preparation? Aren't we taking these tests so we will know what we need to learn to succeed on the SAP tests?"

"Yes, but if we don't succeed on the practice tests, we won't succeed on the tests next spring."

"I have a good staff here, Dr. Saucier. They will teach the curriculum and the students will be ready in April."

"You may be willing to take a chance on that, Bob, but I am not."

"What do you want us to do?"

"Brockton-McGill has SCRUTINY practice tests that can be taken in our computer labs or on the classroom Smartboards if the labs are full."

A long pause followed, then Stevenson spoke, "You're saying that you want us to take practice tests to practice for the practice tests?"

"Yes."

"That's teaching to the test. That's the last thing we want to do."

"No, Bob, it is what we have to do. If the tests are designed to show what we know about math and reading, then if we teach what is on the test our students will know enough to succeed."

"Enough to succeed on this kind of test, but not when they get out into the real world."

Abigail grew angrier as the conversation continued. "Just do what you are told."

As her conversation ended, the cell vibrated once more. Diandra was texting. "I won't b hom for dner."

Abigail hated her daughter's texting shorthand. She could not bring herself to write in less than complete words and sentences. "I expect you to be home."

"Out w Rico," Diandra texted.

Abigail seethed. She did not like her daughter's growing relationship with Rico Salazar. She started to text her a stern warning to be home by dinner, but Diandra had already signed off.

Abigail texted her back. "That was rude, young lady."

'Can't talk now, Mom," Diandra texted. "Im n class."

***

To all appearances, Tollivar was not the most organized teacher. His lesson plans were always well thought out, though he possessed that innate ability veteran teachers have of turning on a dime and heading in a different direction when a lesson wasn't working.

When it came to his lessons, he was always prepared, but he took nowhere near as much care with his desk or his classroom. Books and papers were strewn about on and around his desk. It would take a year for a substitute to figure out where everything was. It never took Tollivar more than a few seconds to find anything he needed. It took him far longer to prepare for a substitute.

He glanced up at the digital clock. 6:18. School had been over for three hours and he was still leaving instructions for his substitute for a simple essay assignment. He hated any day when he was not in his classroom.

"Knock, knock." Tollivar jumped. He was not used to anyone else being around the school this late.

"You need to get home, Walt," Kayla said.

"You're here a bit late yourself."

"I didn't want to take any papers home with me. New rule."

"It's a good rule."

"I take it you're going to the Mark Masters seminar tomorrow."

Tollivar nodded.

"They didn't send me. I get to stay and give the SCRUTINY."

"They are sending twenty-five teachers."

"You're kidding. No, you're not kidding."

"Twenty-five teachers from each school building and on the day we're giving the SCRUTINY tests. We have 12 schools in this district. That's 300 teachers out of class.

"Why did we send four teachers and Dr. Saucier to see this guy in Dallas if we were just going to bring him here to talk to everyone else? We spent a couple of thousand to send them there and pay for their food and lodging; we're paying $10,000 for him to come here. Three hundred substitutes at $100 a day. That's $30,000."

"Plus, we're renting a building and paying for meals for everyone."

"So by the time this is over, the taxpayers are out close to $50,000. And then I have to be gone again the next day."

"You're kidding!"

"No. It's my first appearance as Teacher of the Year, at a Chamber of Commerce dinner."

"And they are wanting you to be gone all day?"

"I have to go to the admin building in the morning to prepare."

"And in the afternoon?"

"I would imagine I will be doing even more preparation to make sure I didn't forget anything that I learned in the morning."

"I'm sorry I got you into this."

Tollivar was, too, but when he saw the regret in her eyes, he couldn't let her know just how much he hated it. "No, don't worry, Kayla." He almost said, "I know you meant well," but he did not want her to feel guilty.

"It will be all right. I'm looking forward to it."

Kayla laughed. "You liar."

"Not too convincing, was I?"

"No, but it was a good try."

"I'm heading out for some ice cream. I could use some company."

"I can't Walt. I'm meeting Tony for drinks."

"Maybe some other time."

"I'd like that." She started to leave, and then turned, "Walt, I nominated you for Teacher of the Year because I know you are the man for the job. I know you don't need or want the hassle, but we need you."

It almost made Walt happy to be Teacher of the Year.

Almost.

CHAPTER TEN

In her brief time as a teacher, Kayla Newman had learned a trick or two about classroom management. Before she was handed a classroom of her own, she had been given the opportunity to observe master teachers in action.

One thing she learned quickly: Different strategies worked for different teachers. Kayla had seen some teachers who brooked no nonsense and were almost never challenged. A quick stare, a rapid gesture were enough to quiet the room.

Others, including Walter Tollivar, handled their classes in a more amiable fashion, almost like holding a conversation with the students. At times, there was noise, but it was almost always the type of noise that went hand in hand with learning.

Kayla knew she would never be a strict disciplinarian so that was the type of class she aspired to teach. At first, it had not been easy. When you look more like a student than a teacher, you are generally treated more like a student, and there were times, more than she cared to remember, that she wore her heart on her sleeve and the students quickly realized they had hurt her feelings. That, of course, is when teenagers pounce.

And this was looking like one of those days. In the back of the room, she saw a pair of dice flying across the floor, accompanied by a cry of "Boxcars."

On the right side of the room, a boyfriend and girlfriend were loudly going through the process of becoming an ex-boyfriend and girlfriend.

Even in the front of the room, three girls were loudly carrying on a conversation about the proper techniques for oral sex, a conversation that was attracting listeners across the room.

"Just like a popsicle," one girl said.

"I always liked popsicles."

Kayla put her hands to her side and quickly gauged the areas of concern. She was supposed to be starting the second SCRUTINY test and she couldn't get anyone to listen to her.

She took a deep breath, then another. She had watched teachers who could dive right in and handle a situation like this without breaking a sweat. She was not one of them.

"Class," she said, attempting to remain calm. The noise continued unabated.

"Class," she said again, and when the noise seemed to increase, she raised her voice slightly and said, "If you will clear your desks and get your popsicles out, I will hand you your tests."

Kayla had no idea what she had said, but the class picked up on it and laughed.

And even worse, two seniors in the back of the room had their "popsicles" out.

It was all Kayla could do to keep from crying, and she was able to for several seconds, but then the dam broke.

It took 15 minutes before Kayla was able to hand out the test booklets and give instructions to the students on how to bubble in the test answers and how to fill in their names, addresses, and school numbers on the back of the booklets.

"Why the hell are we wasting our freaking time with these tests?" a boy in the back said.

"The school district is requiring us to take them to prepare for the SAP tests," Kayla said.

"You'd have to be a SAP to take these tests," he said.

Another boy said, "Well, you're about to take it, you sap."

"Take it back."

And before Kayla could do anything, one boy dived on the other and the fists were flying.

"Boys, boys!" she said. All it took was one blow for one of the boys to start bleeding from the mouth, while the other was quickly blessed with what would soon be a black eye.

"Boys!"

"I'll push the buzzer, Miss Newman," a student named Nick, who was normally not helpful, said.

The maddening high-pitched sound was followed by "Yes?"

The student yelled, "Send the cop down here, they're fucking killing each other."

"Nick!"

"What's your problem, Miss Newman? That ought to get Officer Karl down here quick."

That much was true, she had to admit.

Thirty minutes later, after Officer Karl took the students to the office, Kayla was finally able to get the test started. She decided to do her best to avoid offending the boys who were still rolling craps in the back of the room. Between rolls of the dice, they were diligently bubbling in their answers.

Kayla was just starting to calm down, when the door opened and the two combatants who had been removed just a half hour earlier returned, accompanied by Officer Karl.

"Let me know if these boys cause you any problems, Miss Newman," Officer Karl said. Kayla had forgotten that both the principal and the assistant principal were at the Franklin Heights Family Y listening to a motivational speaker. All Kayla could do was nod. The words wouldn't come out.

The boys, though they didn't seem to have learned anything from their trip to the office, plopped down in their seats.

"I'll get you after school," one said.

"Not unless I turn my back."

'You want a piece of me?'

"Cort, Ricky, stop it!" Kayla shouted. Then she had an idea. "Boys, take it outside."

"Are you serious?"

"Dead serious. Take it outside. After you finish the tests."

For some reason, and Kayla couldn't figure out why, the approach worked. And the SCRUTINY test ran smoothly- until Kayla saw three boys challenging her with loaded popsicles.

"Boys, please put those things back in your pants," she said, in a voice barely above a whisper.

"Aw, c'mon, Miss Newman. I bet you didn't have breakfast." She walked to the other side of the room.

During the last school year, fights, indecent exposure, use of obscene language and gambling in the classroom were all offenses, which would draw out-of-school suspensions.

Now no one was sent home. The edict had been handed down- the students must be kept in school at all costs. A student who is sent home could very well be a student who did not return to school.

And something like that would definitely pull the graduation rate down.

***

"This guy is good," Tollivar said, shocked that the words were coming from his mouth. The school district had reserved the banquet room at the Franklin Heights Y for guest speaker Mark Masters.

Masters was a principal at a Philadelphia school that had seen a dramatic increase in test scores. Naturally, that led to a bestselling book (among educators, at least), *Even My Kids Can Learn*, and a thriving career as a lecturer. No one had paid much attention when his old school's scores went down almost immediately after he left, and, in fact, had dropped slightly the final year he was in charge.

But, as Tollivar had noted, Mark Masters was a powerful speaker. He was so good Tollivar was almost distracted from his claustrophobia. Almost.

Sadly, Tollivar found himself seated at the same table as Abigail Saucier, who was paying complete attention to the speaker.

Then Mark Masters said something that made everyone in the room take notice. "What we have to remember is that standardized tests are important. No doubt about that. They are important, but they are not the be all and end all of education. The most important thing in education is not to blow the top off the state tests, though that was certainly nice when we did it at my old school.

"The most important thing is to give each child the tools to succeed."

"He's right," Tollivar said to no one in particular.

And for the rest of the day, Tollivar took notes as Mark Masters outlined how he had turned his school into one of the most successful in Pennsylvania. His ideas included collaboration time for teachers when they could actually talk about what needed to be done to help students learn.

"He's right," Tollivar said, again addressing no one at his table.

When it was time for a break in the program, Tollivar said to his principal, "This is nowhere near as bad as I thought it was going to be."

"He's a good speaker and he has practiced what he preaches," Robert Stevenson said.

"And we are going to do things the Mark Masters way," Abigail Saucier said. "Excuse me, gentlemen. I need to talk to Mr. Masters."

As soon as she was gone, Stevenson said. "Don't be fooled, Walt. We are not going to do the things the Mark Masters way. We will do things the Abigail Saucier way. Why do you think we are taking the SCRUTINY tests today and six other times during the school year? I guarantee you Mark Masters never did anything like that."

When Abigail returned, she handed Tollivar several sheets of paper, stapled together.

"What's this?" he asked.

"Your speech for the Chamber meeting."

"But I planned on writing something."

"I am saving you the problem, Mister Tollivar."

As Mark Masters resumed speaking, Tollivar read through the pages of his speech, mouth dropping open as he read. Finally, he took his ink pen and scrawled across the top "Mein Kampf."

"How can I be Teacher of the Year and believe in something like this? he thought. And once those thoughts entered his head, he felt a wave of anxiety flow through him and as he once again became cognizant of the number of people in the conference room, the shaking began.

***

The three hours giving the SCRUTINY tests were the longest three hours of Kayla Newman's life. When the tests ended and students were dismissed for lunch, she made her way to the teacher's lounge.

As usual, the Three Amigos, veteran teachers who were inching their way toward retirement and still using their lesson plans from 25 years earlier, were seated around the table offering their opinions on anything that had to do with the school.

The two women, Mary Ann Montgomery, the health and sex education teacher, though from the looks of her she had never learned much about either, and Cynthia Clarkson, a science teacher, had been friends since their first day at Franklin Heights, 27 years earlier. The third Amigo, Cletis Darnell, had been teaching math at Franklin Heights for 18 years.

"These damned computers and Smart boards," Cletis said.

"What's your problem, Cletis? Mary Ann said. "You don't use computers anyway."

"And why should I? What do computers have to do with teaching math?"

Kayla bit her tongue. She was always tempted to say something, but she did want to get on the wrong side of the Three Amigos. They were deeply entrenched in union politics, though they generally used that close proximity to power to punish rather than to help their fellow teachers.

All Kayla wanted to do was to use the microwave to heat her soup, and then take it back to her room. She did not want to get dragged into a Three Amigos conversation.

"What's your problem, Cletis?" Mary Ann repeated.

"It's this Technology Leadership Seminar they're making me take. Why should I waste my time learning something new when I am so close to retirement?"

"You are so right," Cynthia said, as Mary Ann nodded in agreement. "And if it is supposed to be a leadership seminar, then why is everyone having to take it? Why don't they just teach a few of them and let them handle all of the technology?"

Kayla prayed for the sound of the bell signifying that her soup was heated.

Oh, no! Her heart began to pound. They were looking at her. They were going to drag her into the conversation. But the soup was still heating.

"Damn that technology," Kayla said, before anyone could address her. She actually loved technology, but she hated arguing, especially with the Three Amigos.

The bell sounded. Soup was on. "Have a good day?" she said politely, as she took her soup and exited.

As she started down the hall, she could hear Cletis saying, "For a new teacher, she's all right."

Maybe it would have been better to have been on their bad side, she thought.

"How'd things go with the Amigos?" Tony Peterson asked.

"They're happy being unhappy."

"Same as usual. I thought that teacher's lounge stuff was just something they said to scare us when we were in college."

"Let me get my sandwich and I'll join you."

"All right."

When he returned, he took a good look at Kayla. "It looks like you've had a tough day."

I am not going to cry, she thought.

"I take it the SCRUTINY tests didn't go very well."

I am not going to cry.

"It's going to get worse."

"How could it get worse?" she said, continuing her resolve not to cry.

"Word came down from Dr. Saucier at admin. We have to pull up our scores on these practice tests, so we are going to use the Brockton-McGill website to prepare quizzes that will get us ready for the SCRUTINY tests."

"No. You can't be serious."

"Dead serious."

"We're going to take tests to prepare us to take tests to prepare us to take tests?"

"Bingo."

And for the sixth or seventh time that day, Kayla had lost count, she began crying.

CHAPTER ELEVEN

Tollivar discovered Abigail Saucier's plan to increase the emphasis on the SCRUTINY tests when he read it in the text of the speech he was supposed to deliver to the Franklin Heights Chamber of Commerce.

"This is a nightmare," he said, not realizing he had said it out loud. He was seated between Abigail Saucier and Carlton Dunn at the head table, with the three surrounded by the cream of Franklin Heights' business community.

"What's a nightmare, Mister Tollivar?" Abigail asked.

"I'm just not sure I can do justice to this speech," he said, saying the first words that popped into his head. The meal was the traditional rubber chicken, with potato salad and baked beans.

The program began with the minutes from the previous Chamber meeting, followed by recognition of some businesses that had been open for 10, 15, 20, and 25 years. The Chamber president introduced Carlton Dunn and Abigail, who received a generous round of applause.

"And now our guest speaker for the evening. We all appreciate the work our teachers are doing to mold our young people, though I have no idea why we would want moldy young people." He paused, waiting for laughter that never came.

"And this is the best among the best. The teacher of the year for the Franklin Heights Unified School District- Mr. Walter Tollivar."

Tollivar stood and acknowledged the warm applause. He picked up the speech that had been prepared for him by Abigail Saucier, then slowly, deliberately, put it in his back pocket.

It may have been Abigail Saucier's plan for the Teacher of the Year to praise the programs she had installed in the school district, but it wasn't his. If the words were going to come from his lips, they were going to be his words.

***

"Forgive me if I am a little nervous," Tollivar began. "This is the first time I have spoken in front of a crowd like this in years. Normally, the people I speak to have more important things on their minds, like who's dating whom and what's on sale at the mall." There were a few polite chuckles.

"Being teacher of the year for the Franklin Heights Unified School District is a great honor, yet it is one that could just as easily be given to dozens of deserving teachers."

Tollivar took the microphone out of the stand and sauntered out into the crowd. "How many of you had your lives affected in a positive way by a classroom teacher?"

Hands began to shoot up across the room.

"So did I," he said. "Her name was Janet Maxwell and she was a speech teacher. I wasn't much interested in speech; it was one of those classes they made you take at my high school. She was a new teacher in the school system and she had that kind of I Love Lucy hair- do you remember that?" Several of the audience members nodded.

"That was not the class for me," Tollivar said. "I was not one of those who had an affinity for public speaking; in fact, I had a noticeable speech impediment that kept me from talking much at all. And our school did not have a speech therapist.

"But Mrs. Maxwell, that dear wonderful woman, worked with me. She worked with me in class, she worked with me after school, and before long the problems I had were a thing of the past.

"Mrs. Maxwell believed in me, but not any more than she believed in the rest of her students. That is what being a classroom teacher is all about. Without Mrs. Maxwell, I would not be standing before you today. I would definitely not be standing in front of a classroom full of your sons and daughters five days a week." Tollivar approached the front table. "Mister Mayor, do you have a teacher who helped you become the community leader you are today?"

The mayor, never a stranger to a microphone, took it from Tollivar and told a story about a teacher who had affected his life. After that, Tollivar worked the room, gathering testimonials from one businessperson after another, who shared the effect classroom teachers had in making them the successes they had become.

After the final testimonial, Tollivar said, "Being Teacher of the Year has given me an opportunity to remind you, not only about the wonderful things we have going on in the Franklin Heights Unified School District, but also about the hard working, dedicated people who care enough about your children to make them the focal point of their lives. Thank you for listening."

As he returned to his seat, he placed the microphone back on the stand and acknowledged the sustained applause.

Carlton Dunn turned to Abigail Saucier. "You never said he was this good."

"Mister Tollivar is a man of many surprises," she said, as Tollivar made his way back to his seat. "I'm not sure I like that."

CHAPTER TWELVE

NOVEMBER

After two months of the school year, one thing had become painfully obvious to Abigail- the school district was headed toward disastrous results on the SAP tests. The SCRUTINY tests were not looking good for the elementary and middle schools, and the high school was looking even worse.

And the blame for that could be placed squarely at the doorstep of Carlton Dunn.

The new superintendent's program to increase the graduation rate was creating the risk of having SAP scores drop to their lowest levels ever.

"What can we do about this?" Abigail asked Stanley Kramer and the district curriculum director Jane VanCleave."

Kramer asked, "What have we done in the past?"

"Well, I am not sure I should-"

Abigail interrupted, "Go ahead, Jane. It won't leave this room."

"This was usually the time of the year we began encouraging students to leave school."

Kramer looked stunned. "We were doing that?"

"Of course we were doing that," Abigail said. "Don't be naïve. Everybody does it."

VanCleave continued, "Any student who received disciplinary referrals and did not appear capable of helping us on the SAP tests was given an out-of-school suspension and we kept doing it until the students did not show up."

"But wouldn't those students count against us with the state?"

"Some of them enrolled at other high schools; some of them were home schooled."

"Those kids were homeschooled?" Kramer asked.

"As far as we knew; the state never checked."

We also encouraged students who became pregnant or missed a large number of days to believe it would be wiser to come back to school the next year or to get their GEDs. Not very many of them ever came back."

"And why aren't we doing these things this year?" Kramer asked. "You know how important those tests are. If we don't reach our yearly progress goal, we can be declared a failing school and lose funding."

"What the hell do you want us to do, Stanley?" Abigail screamed. "The pregnant girls come right back after they deliver their babies because they can leave their children at our new daycare center. We are even getting teen mothers from other school districts.

"We are not even allowed to discipline the students, much less to kick them out. Dunn has it fixed where for the first time every malcontent in Franklin Heights wants to come to school because it is the 'cool' place to be. The inmates are running the asylum.

"We have drugs, sex, alcohol, outside the school, in the stairwells, in the hallways, and in the classrooms."

"A regular Smartboard Jungle," Kramer said.

"We have to do something with that Smartboard Jungle," Abigail said. Her cell phone vibrated. She glanced quickly into her lap. It was a text message from Diandra. "Hot sex tonight, Mom. Don't wait up."

What in the world was she going to do with that girl? "I think I have an answer to our problem," she said. She texted Diandra. "Stop by my office tonight. Bring Rico Salazar with you."

"What's your idea?" Kramer asked.

"I'm going to take a page out of Dr. Dunn's book. I don't know if it will work or not, but my daughter's boyfriend is going to bring up test scores at Franklin Heights High School."

***

It was one week after the meeting in Abigail Saucier's office that Rico Salazar began adding an extra $1,000 to his paycheck every month, in addition to being given money to use for other purposes.

"Where's my money?" one student asked as Salazar came into the room.

"Word gets around fast." Salazar pulled two wrinkled 20-dollar bills out of his pocket. "Show me your math test."

The other boy proudly exhibited his test.

"All right, my man," he said, handing him the 20s.

Students kept collecting their money as Tollivar approached. He quickly ascertained what was going on. "You have to be kidding me. We're paying students to do well on tests. We are using taxpayer money to bribe teenagers?"

"It's the fucking free enterprise system," Salazar said.

"Yeah," Rock parroted, "the fucking free enterprise system."

Tollivar walked away, a disgusted look on his face.

"He must not like free enterprise," Chris said.

"It's the fucking free enterprise system," Rock said again.

"We're past that," Salazar said, laughing. "My woman approaches."

At one time there had been a dress code at Franklin Heights High School, and, there still was one, but under the new laws of the jungle there was no way to enforce it, something that Diandra Saucier liked.

Diandra was with her mother. "Just bringing your daughter to school today, Abby, or are you ready for another quickie?"

Abigail ignored the remark. "How is our plan going?"

"Grades are up, Abby. They should put us in the White House. There wouldn't be any children left behind. Diandra slid over to Salazar and put one arm on his shoulder and the palm of her hand flat on his crotch.

"Diandra."

"Like mother, like daughter," Salazar said.

"I beg your pardon?"

"Like mother, like daughter," Rock repeated.

"I heard what he said."

"Then why did you act like you didn't? I don't understand women."

Abigail glared at Salazar. "What did you mean by that?"

Diandra answered the question. "You know what he means by that, mother. You spent a lot of time working under Dr. Feinberg. And I do mean under Dr. Feinberg."

"Abigail!"

"Don't try to deny it."

"She's got you, Abby."

"And you told this scum about it?"

"Hey! That's no way to talk about your future son-in-law!"

A look of horror spread across Abigail's face.

"Had you going, didn't I?"

"Don't worry, Mom," Diandra said. "We're just screwing- a lot- like he said, like mother, like daughter. " She put her hand back on Salazar's crotch. "Baby want to play?"

"Diandra!"

"Don't worry, Mom. We'll wait until after school."

"She's on the pill," Rock said.

"Did I remember to take that?"

"Diandra!"

"Yes, I did. Don't worry, Mom. Go back to your office."

"We'll take care of things around here," Salazar said, kissing Diandra and putting his hands on her rear.

"Don't wait up, Mom," Diandra called as her mother left the school, her face flushed with anger.

***

It was not the way Kayla Newman liked to spend her planning period. The school district had paid $10,000 for a university professor to instruct teachers on a new process called learning practice inventory or LPI, for short.

Since her planning period was third hour, Kayla normally reviewed what had taken place during the first two hours and made any needed adjustments to her lesson plans. When things were working smoothly, she called parents of students who were not turning in their work, a difficult task since most parents were not home or available at work, and many students had provided the school with numbers that were either fictitious or had been disconnected by the time a teacher or anyone else from the school called.

But with the new LPI initiative started by Abigail Saucier, Kayla had to give up her planning period for three consecutive days.

Under LPI, Kayla or the other teachers who had gone through the training and were also losing their planning periods waited until 10 minutes passed at the beginning of the hour to give teachers a chance to get students settled then stepped into the classrooms and with one quick glance were supposed to determine the students' level of engagement.

The engagement level was rated on a scale of one to six with six being the ultimate goal. At five and six, students were involved in research, student-led discussions, in fact, just about anything that was initiated by students, rather than teachers. The idea behind LPI was that the best kind of learning only took place when the students did it themselves. Teachers were simply the facilitators.

A teacher leading a class in a discussion or lecturing students received a four rating, while students doing busy work that had been given to them by a teacher, no matter how high the educational value, received a three.

The lowest rating, one, went to classes in which the students were not engaged and in which no learning was taking place.

Teachers were told LPI was not an evaluation, but no one bought into that. Why would the district spend so much money sending the teachers to the seminars if the results were not going to be used to judge teachers?

The teachers had been told to leave their doors unlocked to allow the evaluators access without them having to interrupt the class, but many of the teachers simply ignored the request or forgot.

Kayla did not want to knock on the door, so it took three classrooms before she found one with the door unlocked. She opened the door, trying to make as little noise as possible. That plan never worked. It did not matter how chaotic a classroom was, any time the door opened, the students turned that way.

It was obvious the chemistry teacher, who had been in the middle of a lecture, was irritated by Kayla's entrance. He stopped in mid-sentence. "Yes?"

"No, please go ahead."

"What can I do for you?"

Kayla knew what was going on. Terry Dreyfuss was one of those who felt threatened by LPI and since he could not take out his frustration on Abigail Saucier, he planned to take it out on Kayla.

"I'm just observing."

"Mmm. I'm observing her," a senior said, making the comment sound as lecherous as possible.

This was not the way LPI was supposed to work. He was supposed to continue teaching. Kayla felt all eyes in the classroom were on her, and in fact they were.

She started backing toward the door. "Why don't you hold the door for Miss Newman, Henry?" Dreyfuss said.

"That's not necessary."

"Of course it is. I wouldn't want to make one of my fellow teachers feel unwelcome." Before Henry could reach the door, Kayla was in the hallway.

Though no learning had been taking place in the classroom for most of the time Kayla had been there, she jotted down a 4 on the scoring sheet. It was obvious Dreyfuss was lecturing when she entered the room, and most likely had resumed lecturing already.

As Kayla prepared to walk into the next classroom, she heard angry voices coming from the stairs by the media center.

"You don't fool around on me, bitch," a tall senior with a shaved head adorned with a dragon tattoo, was telling a tiny freshman girl.

"I didn't, Josh, I swear."

"You fucking liar," he said, slapping her.

"Stop it," Kayla shouted, but she had no idea how she was going to make that happen. She was only slightly bigger than the freshman and would be no match for the young man.

"Stay out of it, bitch. This is between me and her."

Kayla's heart pounded as she tried to figure out what to do. No one was in that area of the hall. Officer Karl was probably on the other side of the school building since he was presenting drug awareness videos to the health classes.

"No, get your hands off her," Kayla said, and surprisingly, that was just what the young man did, but not quite in the way Kayla wanted. Josh, whose last name escaped Kayla since she did not have him in any of her classes, tossed the freshman to the floor like a rag doll and slowly moved toward Kayla.

"Stand back," she said, but her words did not faze him at all. Kayla began backing up and soon found her back to the wall. She was trapped.

Kayla had hoped the freshman would run to get help, but the girl was too frightened to move. "Get help," she said, and she was going to scream, but Josh put his hand over her mouth. "Now you're going to get exactly what you deserve," and he ripped the top of her blouse with his free hand.

He pushed Kayla roughly against the wall and a loud, screeching sound filled the hallways. Josh had pushed her against the fire alarm.

It took only a few seconds before students poured out of the class-rooms and into the hallway. Josh turned Kayla loose and ran like the rest of them- outside the building, many of them planning not to return until the next day. Planned fire drills were one thing; it was hard to escape during those, but anytime someone pulled the alarm, it was vacation time.

Kayla did not follow the students out of the building. She slumped in front of a locker.

She remembered the name of the young man who had assaulted her, Josh Mason- the same Josh Mason who had been expelled from Franklin Heights High the previous year, after he had beaten a girl behind the bleachers at a football game, the same Josh Mason who, thanks to Carlton Dunn's graduation initiative, could now use the hallways as his own private hunting preserve.

**

"Are we ready to have a damned meeting yet?" Leron Hundley asked no one in particular.

The conversations continued around the coach as he reached into the box of jelly doughnuts thoughtfully provided by the instructional coach.

"Why the hell don't we talk about some students for a change and what we can do for them?"

The conversations continued unabated.

"Does it take two months of meetings for us to learn how to have meetings," he asked.

For a third time, there was no reply.

"My wife's having another baby and it ain't mine."

"That's a shame, Leroy," Michael O'Leary said.

"She's not pregnant, I just wanted to see if I could get through to any-body. Why in the hell are we here at 7 a.m.? I have work to do in the gym!"

O'Leary ignored the question.

"Why is it I have to talk about my wife getting pregnant to get anyone to answer me?"

"Your wife's pregnant?" Kayla asked.

"No, no, my wife is not pregnant. Well, at least she wasn't the last time we talked."

"You and Darla are going to have a baby, Leron," the principal said.

"No."

"Keep him talking about the baby," O'Leary said. "We've already heard everything he has to say about these meetings."

In a couple of seconds, the instructional coach, one had been hired for each building by Abigail Saucier, raised her hand, which was supposed to be the universal signal for silence.

The universal signal was ignored, so the woman, who had been a classroom teacher for 24 years, yelled, "If I could have your attention."

The room quieted. There are few sadder sights than a classroom full of teachers getting in trouble.

"Before we can truly have effective meetings," the woman said, "we have to develop the proper mindset."

"We have been having meetings all of our lives," Leron mumbled. There were nods all around his table.

The learning coach continued, "But before we begin…"

"We're going to have a damned team builder," Leron said. He stood. "We're already a damned team, woman. We're all united to teach children and to someday hold meetings to help those children if Dr. Saucier will ever let us."

Not knowing quite how to react to the interruption, the instructional coach said, "I want you to number off from one to six, starting with you, Mrs. Miller." As the teachers reluctantly counted, the coach said, "This is a fun activity I first learned when I was teaching third grade."

"So now we're all damned third graders," Leron said, slamming his fist against the table. "Any more of those jelly doughnuts left?"

As the activity began, teams of adult teachers, who had spent years earning degrees that put them in the ranks of a once-revered profession, tried to move balloons in relay style from one teacher to the next, without using their hands. Despite his opposition to team builders and to meetings to learn how to hold meetings in general, the competitive fires began burning for Leron, who was loudly exhorting his team to victory.

"You can't let us get beat by a damned special ed teacher!" he shouted.

"It's a game, Leroy, it's just a game," O'Leary said, scooting under the green balloon and bumping it with his head toward Kayla.

The balloon was descending toward the floor far too fast. She lunged forward, trying to get under it, but it hit her shoulder and fell to the floor.

"Now we've got to start all over again," Leron sighed. "We're getting beat by a bunch of special ed teachers."

Kayla looked at the balloon lying on the floor, and then bolted for the door.

Tony Peterson started to follow her, until Tollivar stepped in front of him. "I'll go."

Peterson started to protest, then nodded.

Tollivar checked the hallway, but didn't see Kayla. A few moments later, he noticed that the door to Kayla's classroom was shut. He knocked.

"Kayla."

"Go away!"

"I'm not going away."

"I can't talk about it, Walt."

"Then just let me sit with you. You don't have to say a word."

Tollivar heard the key being placed in the lock and saw the doorknob turning. For a moment after the door opened, Kayla stood with her head facing the floor. When she raised her head, it was obvious she had been crying. After an awkward silence, Walter put his arms around her and she fell against him, the tears flowing again.

"It wasn't the balloon," she said.

"I know. What happened yesterday?"

She told the story of what had happened during the LPI, her words pouring out for several minutes as she never stopped to take a breath. When she finished, she sighed, and said, "I don't think I have what it takes to be a teacher. I am scared to death every moment I am in this building.

"How long is it going to be before someone gets killed?"

CHAPTER THIRTEEN

W e are in the middle of a new era at Franklin Heights High School," Carlton Dunn said, as he ushered reporters for the local television stations through the hallways.

"Take a look at these bright, eager young people. Just a year ago, many of these youngsters would be walking the streets, condemned to a life of poverty and prison, a world full of despair and desperation. Now, they will be crossing the stage when we hold commencement ceremonies and picking up passports to prosperity. Did you get all of that?"

"I missed the first part," one photographer said. Dunn repeated it word for word.

"Turn your attention toward this hallway. The young man who is approaching has turned his life around. Rico, come here."

Rico Salazar, hands in his pockets, and as usual, accompanied by Rock and Chris, said, "What's shaking, Doc?"

"Rico Salazar was a hoodlum, a dope dealer, the scum of the earth."

"I was scum," Rico said, overdramatizing it a bit.

"He was scum," Rock repeated.

"And how have you changed, Mr. Salazar?" one of the reporters asked.

"It's all this education," Rico said, scratching his forehead. "Dr. Dunn was right. I was a hoodlum, a dope dealer, I was worse than the scum of the earth."

"He was worse," Rock said.

"And what has changed? the reporter asked.

"Education, man. In six months, I'll be a hoodlum, a dope dealer, and scum of the earth with a diploma."

Dunn smiled. "And that's not all is it, Rock?"

Rock looked at him, not picking up on what Dunn was saying.

"And that's not all is it, Rock?"

It clicked. Rock smiled with pride as he remembered the message he had been taught earlier that day.

"Don't forget to face out our Checkbook page."

CHAPTER FOURTEEN

DECEMBER

Y ou are joking. You have to be joking." "What makes you think I am joking, Mr. Stevenson. Your SCRUTI-NY scores are terrible and your practice scores for the SCRUTINY are even worse."

"Dr. Saucier, you're talking about practice tests for practice tests."

"And your point is?"

"You already have us teaching to the test; you can't be serious about this. "

"Mr. Stevenson, you are fully aware of what is going on at this high school. Thanks to our new change in policy, Franklin Heights High has become the home to the criminals, drug users, degenerates, and malcontents who would have been shoved out on the streets last year. We are not going to be able to do anything about it, so we have to find a way to bring their test scores up."

"Then please let us teach. We can't have more testing. The teachers are already on edge."

"The teachers," Abigail said, taking a long, deliberate pause, "are going to do whatever we tell them to do. That is in their contracts. As long as we have a rock solid curriculum, we can bring in other teachers who will do what needs to be done."

"Dr. Saucier, teachers are the indispensable ones in this school system."

"No, Mr. Stevenson, teachers are dispensable, and so are principals. It is the curriculum that is indispensable. Now, if we can get down to business."

"This is going to take every bit of the joy out of learning."

"We are not judged on the basis of how much joy our students are getting. I don't care if they are miserable, or if the teachers are miserable as long as we bring up our scores on the SAP tests."

Stevenson sighed. "What do you want us to do?"

"Beginning this month, we will start taking the new SAP PREP tests on Tuesday and Wednesday mornings during the third week of each month. These tests are designed to find the students who are getting left behind by the SCRUTINY tests."

"So we will take the SAP Prep, to prepare us for the practice SCRUTINY tests which prepare us for the SCRUTINY tests which prepare us for the SAP tests."

"Now you've got it."

"Is there anything else?"

"Yes, you need to choose six teachers to send to the state capital Thursday and Friday for SAP PREP training."

"Six teachers? But we already have eight teachers who will be attending the STAR meeting Thursday, two teachers who are on leave, and we have three more going to the LPI training Friday. How are students going to learn enough to pass these tests if they don't have their regular classroom teachers?"

"That's why we pay good money for trained substitutes. If your teachers can prepare decent lesson plans, the students will learn on those days when they are out of the classroom. Oh, I will also be taking Mister Tollivar with me to the Kiwanis Club meeting Friday. He will need to be at the admin building at 10 a.m. and he should be back by 2."

"Have you run this past him?"

"He is the Teacher of the Year, Mister Stevenson. You act like he needs to be in the classroom."

"Sorry, Dr. Saucier. I don't know what gets into me."

As she left Stevenson's office, Abigail nearly ran into Rico Salazar.

"Abby," he said, as if he were greeting a long lost friend. "Just the woman I wanted to see. I need cash."

"You always need cash. And you are not getting results."

Salazar put his hand on Abigail's shoulder. She had never realized just how scary this young man could be. "Please take your hand off my shoulder."

"And all of this time I thought you had a thing for me, Abby. You know, like daughter, like mother. I like the daughter." He put his hand under her chin. "I think I could like the mother, too."

"You'll get your cash."

"Good, by the way, I disabled the surveillance camera in this hallway a few days ago. It was interfering with business, if you know what I mean."

"So?"

"You don't have to worry about anyone seeing me doing this?"

Before Abigail knew what was happening, this young man, more than 20 years her junior, was kissing her…and it was the best kiss she had had in years.

"No, we can't do this."

"Sure we can, Abby. And we will. " She pulled away from Salazar and ran down the hall as quickly as she could. Her face was flushed and her heart was pounding.

She could hear Salazar's laughter echoing from the hallway. She was so flustered by this turn of events, though, that she failed to notice that Diandra had seen everything.

***

Abigail peeled out of the high school parking lot, nearly hitting a pick-up truck she had failed to see coming around the corner. Though it was the middle of the school day, she had to go home. Every once in a while, she needed that "lazy, low life no good husband" to provide her with a break from a frustrating day and this was one time she was happy he was nowhere near to landing a job. It took only a few minutes for her to reach her home since she only lived four blocks from the high school.

She turned her key in the door as quietly as possible. She knew her husband would still be in bed. He rarely got up before noon on weekdays unless he was golfing. And as far as she knew, he was not golfing today since he had not returned home until well after midnight the previous night.

To save time, Abigail began removing articles of clothing as she headed toward their bedroom. She was down to a pair of blue panties and her heels, just the way Bob liked it. It had been a long time since Abigail had felt so horny in the middle of the day.

She opened the bedroom door just in time to see that what she wanted to start, her husband was already finishing. The bed cover and sheets were strewn across the floor, as well as both pillows. Bob was naked, lying on his back on the bed, as their neighbor, a 30-year old divorcee was riding him for all she was worth.

The woman was oblivious to Abigail's entry, emitting several high-pitched sounds that made her sound more like the object of a greased pig scramble at the county fair than a woman in the throes of an orgasm.

"I'll be right with you, honey," Bob Saucier said.

"You are right with me, Bobby," the woman said.

"No, I was talking to Abigail."

"Abigail?" The woman started to climb off Bob, but he held her fast. "Hold on a second," he said. A few seconds later, he had completed his part of the deal.

"Come on in, honey," Bob said. "There's enough for everybody."

"You bastard, get out of here," she said, and having nothing else handy, she took off one of her heels and threw it at him, bouncing it off the wall behind the bed.

"I've gotta go, Bobby," the woman said.

"I'll call later."

"Get out!" Abigail screamed again.

"Hey, Betty, mind if I take a shower at your place." Bob Saucier grabbed a shirt, a pair of pants and some shoes and followed his lover out the door.

As he left, Abigail stood alone in the bedroom, only her panties and one heel standing between her and nakedness. She had never felt as lonely…or as turned on as she was feeling at that moment. When she heard the front door slam behind her cheating husband, she stepped over to her bureau, opened her underwear drawer, rummaged through the silken fabric until she found what she wanted, and at this moment, what she desperately needed.

It was thick, black and slightly less than 10 inches long. She kicked off her heel, slipped out of her panties, and then slipped into bed with her plastic partner. Moments later, Bob and the neighbor were forgotten. Abigail closed her eyes, and though it surprised her, she imagined that it was Rico Salazar driving into her over and over and over again until he had her shaking uncontrollably and left her exhausted and totally satisfied.

CHAPTER FIFTEEN

It was a sheepish Rock who knocked on the door to Kayla's classroom shortly after the final bell sounded the end to another school day. "Miss Newman."

"Yes, Clinton?" Kayla was the only teacher who called him by his given name.

"If you're busy, I can come back another time."

"No, please, come on in." Kayla had seen students cower in fear before Rico Salazar's friend and apparent bodyguard, but she had never seen Rock Brennan in quite that way. "Sit down."

Rock planted himself in a seat that was much too small for his football lineman type frame.

"How can I help you, Clinton?"

"I want to learn how to read."

Before Kayla could respond, he said, "I never learned how to read. I tried when I was in first grade, but I didn't get it and no one ever helped me."

How had he ever reached this point, being a high school senior, without knowing how to read?

As if he had read her mind, Rock explained, "People always helped me."

"Helped you?"

"I had people who did my work for me and I would help them take care of their problems," he said, slamming his right fist into the open palm of his left hand, leaving no doubt about just how he dealt with those problems.

"I can put you with a group that helps adults who don't know how to read or have reading problems," Kayla said. "I have the number in my address book."

"Could you help me?"

"I normally don't do that sort of thing."

"I understand. I'm just tired of being dumb."

"You're not dumb, Clinton, and don't let anyone tell you that you are. You didn't let me finish. I normally haven't done tutoring because until a few weeks ago I had been working a second job after school."

"Teachers need that much money?"

"Some of us do," Kayla said, deciding it would be wiser not to explain to Rock how little money teachers make. "Since I don't have the second job any more, I would be happy to help you read. When would you like to start?"

"Whenever you can."

"Give me some time to get some materials together, Clinton. Would you like to start next Monday?"

He nodded. "Thank you, Miss Newman. I won't bother you any more."

"You haven't bothered me at all."

Just before Rock left the room, he turned to Kayla and said, "No one at this school is ever going to mess with you again," and once again he slammed his fist into his palm.

Kayla was no fan of the kind of violence she was beginning to see in the halls of Franklin Heights High School, but hearing Rock say those words made her feel safe for the first time in a long time.

***

Robert Stevenson's tenure as Franklin Heights High School principal ended that same day, as Officer Karl escorted him from the building under orders from Superintendent Carlton Dunn.

"I'm sorry about this, Mister Stevenson," Officer Karl said. "You deserve better than this."

"I'm not taking it personally, Karl. You're just doing your job."

"What did you do to get fired?"

Stevenson smiled. "It's not what I did. It's what I refused to do. I have bent over backwards for the people at admin, but I refuse to lower my standards and this school's standards any more."

As they reached Stevenson's car, Officer Karl said, "I'll see to it you get your stuff."

"Thanks, Karl. Good luck." He added under his breath, "You're going to need it."

***

It didn't take long for Assistant Principal Willis Shantz to implement the changes that Robert Stevenson had refused to make.

The teachers knew Stevenson had done the best he could to protect them from the demands from the central administration office.

After the initial order to keep students in class at whatever cost, no matter what disciplinary problems they were creating had been issued, Stevenson had argued against it, noting that students who were trying to learn would be unable to do so because of the added disruptions in the classroom.

Dunn, through an Abigail Saucier memo, said, "If our teachers don't know how to maintain discipline in their classrooms, maybe we need to find new teachers."

At first, Stevenson followed the orders to the letter as he tried to figure out a way to deal with the chaos that had been created. There was nothing worse to Stevenson's way of thinking than to send a troublemaker back to the same classroom on the same day without meting out some kind of punishment. Not only had the practice increased the disciplinary problems, but it had also demoralized the teachers.

After trying the system for several days and realizing the devastating effect it was having on education at Franklin Heights High, Stevenson tried placing the students in the in-school suspension room as he had always done and hope that no one from the admin building noticed.

Of course, Abigail Saucier had and demanded that the practice be stopped.

Stevenson's next move, borne out of desperation, was to put the student into ISS, but only for the class in which the disturbance had occurred. After a few days, Abigail found an effective way to stop that practice, as well. She transferred the in-school suspension teacher to one of the middle schools, and did not replace him. Stevenson was forced to return the troublemakers to the classes after he had talked to him. He tried talking to them long enough that it would take them into the next hour, but he simply had too many duties to do that often, so the situation continued, worsening with the passing of each day.

Stevenson had always had a reputation as a strong disciplinary principal who was strict but fair. When he had taken the job at Franklin Heights High six years earlier, it had a reputation of being a problem school. It took him just two years to fix those problems, starting with a change in disciplinary policies and then finding a way to improve the classroom management techniques of some of his younger teachers.

After those first two years, the high school's atmosphere had changed and the number one priority was education.

Those changes had all been undercut in just three months by the actions taken by central administration.

The last straw for Stevenson came when he refused to sacrifice the one thing he felt could not be sacrificed, the sanctity of students' grades.

That was one refusal too many and cost Stevenson his job. Willis Shantz, now the acting principal, was too close to retirement to lose his livelihood. He issued the memo that Stevenson had stuck in his desk drawer and ignored:

"As of today," the memo began, "teachers will not issue F grades to any students in their classes. If the students are not making the grade, then the teachers will need to work harder."

Another part of the instructions that Stevenson had refused to follow was not told to the teachers, but Tollivar discovered it when he accidentally opened his electronic gradebook from the previous year.

Grades had been changed.

Students who had flunked his junior classes suddenly received passing grades. Following a hunch, Tollivar checked the grades of the students who had dropped out the previous year, but had returned to Franklin Heights High after being persuaded by Carlton Dunn.

Every one of the students had higher grades- and was back on the path to graduation.

If this continued, Tollivar thought, Carlton Dunn was going to single-handedly ruin the symbol of education that had meant something to generation after generation.

"A Franklin Heights High School diploma means nothing," he said aloud, though he was the only one in the room.

"This madness has to stop."

***

The first fringe benefit from Kayla's new arrangement with Rock came a few days later.

Kayla was called to the office during her planning period. As she left her room, she noticed large numbers of students roaming the halls, a condition that had existed since the beginning of school, but had grown considerably worse in the few days following the firing of Robert Stevenson.

The students, most of whom were wrapped up in their own activities, ignored her but as she neared the office, she saw an obstacle standing in her way. The area by the office was not one of the places the students elected to gather when they were cutting classes. Josh Mason, however, did not worry about anyone interfering with his business. When he skipped class, he had the run of the school.

And he was standing between Kayla and the office.

"We didn't get to finish what we started," he said.

Kayla did not speak. She could not speak.

Mason approached her, trying to maneuver her toward the lockers. There was no chance of Kayla repeating her good luck from the previous encounter. The fire alarm was located in a different part of the hall.

Kayla closed her eyes as she felt Mason pick her up by the shoulders and hold her against the locker. Even though he was only holding her with one hand, he was far too powerful for Kayla to break free.

She heard the unmistakable sound of his zipper coming down and then she felt her skirt being pulled up. This couldn't be happening. Not in the main hallway of a public school building. Even worse, she could hear people roaming the halls. And not one of them was stopping to prevent rape from being committed.

She started to scream, but it took only a few seconds for Mason's hand to clamp over her mouth.

Kayla tried to think about anything else- the papers she was grading, what she had for dinner the previous evening, her childhood. Just please get it over with quickly, she prayed. "No, I can't let this happen," she said, and she raised her knee quickly in an effort to hit Mason in the groin. Though she missed, it distracted him long enough for her to break away. She tried to run, but he had already caught her.

But only for a second.

Kayla felt his hands being pulled forcibly from her shoulders. "Get up," she heard a voice scream, and she recognized Clinton Brennan.

"I said get up," he repeated. Kayla turned and saw Josh Mason crawling backward as her rescuer towered over him. "Get up."

Kayla was thinking thoughts she had never thought before. She wanted to see Josh Mason beaten to a pulp. She wasn't going to do anything to try to stop Rock. Just as Rock picked Mason off the floor, three adults, led by Officer Karl, swept in and stood between the two.

"Come on, fun time's over," Officer Karl said. "Mason, we need to get you to the nurse's office. Are you all right, Miss Newman?"

Kayla nodded.

She watched as Officer Karl escorted Mason to the nurse's office.

"Thank you, Clinton," she said.

"I'm not going to let him hurt you, Miss Newman. I'm not going to let anybody hurt you."

"That's not what I meant. It's just different."

***

After Robert Stevenson had managed to get most of the teachers with negative attitudes transferred out of Franklin Heights High, a small group of teachers started promoting the idea that the faculty was more like a second family. And while Tollivar enjoyed working with his fellow faculty members, he never bought into that concept.

First, it was picnics in the park and softball games, with faculty members who attended bringing their families. That evolved into farewell receptions for retiring teachers, baby showers for pregnant staff members, wedding showers for those who were entering the bonds of holy matrimony and, of course, the annual Christmas party.

Usually, Tollivar sent his apologies and said he could not make it to the events because he was tied up that evening and that was the absolute truth. Sometimes he was tied up in reading a book, other times he was tied up in watching a ball game; a time or two he had even been tied up in taking long naps.

Whatever the social occasion, Tollivar managed to be tied up. Only this time, the organizers of the annual Christmas party played the Teacher of the Year card.

"This is our biggest party," they said. "It won't be family without the Teacher of the Year around."

"But I wasn't there last year!" Tollivar protested.

"You weren't Teacher of the Year last year," they responded and he had no argument against that. Finally, he agreed to make a token appearance at the beginning of the party and then he would quietly slip out some side door, go home, take a long nap, and do everything he could to forget about his second family until classes resumed after Christmas vacation.

Since no one wanted to hold a festive event in a school gymnasium or cafeteria, the faculty party fund, which consisted of contributions solicited every payday, was used to rent a room at Rollo's Pizza Emporium.

By holding the party at Rollo's instead of one of the fancier Franklin Heights restaurants, faculty members who may have been running short on money (and there was always a large number of those) could afford the food. Plus, for those who occasionally (or frequently) wanted to drink something with some alcoholic content, Rollo's offered all the beer and light beer they could handle. Or in the case of a few of the teachers, more than they could handle.

The worst part for Tollivar was the small size of Rollo's meeting rooms. Even though, their pooled money was able to rent two adjacent rooms, the faculty and staff were packed in tightly into the dining area. Tollivar stood in the area that would be used for dancing after the meal. Not many ever danced, but Tollivar was grateful there were enough who did that the open area was necessary.

Every once in a while, a faculty member would venture over to say a hello to Tollivar and indulge in a few words of meaningless conversation. A few wandered over to complain about the things that were going on at the high school, the drugs, the violence, the grade inflation.

"You're Teacher of the Year," one asked. "Why don't you do something?"

Tollivar explained that Teacher of the Year was more of a figurehead position than something of real substance.

It was at that point that Acting Principal Willis Shantz arrived, entering the room with someone who had not been invited- Abigail Saucier.

The room suddenly grew quiet. It had not taken long for the word to get around that Robert Stevenson had been fired because he crossed paths with the assistant superintendent.

She began working the room, telling each person what a wonderful job he or she had been doing and that she wanted to wish all of her teachers a merry Christmas.

Those who had ordered alcoholic beverages kept their distance from their drinks. The teachers did not want to give this woman an excuse to send them to the unemployment line.

Tollivar was hoping he would not be noticed, but after she had shaken hands and exchanged small talk with two groups of teachers she headed directly to where he was standing.

"Mister Tollivar, I hope our Teacher of the Year is planning something nice and relaxing for his holiday break."

"Reading and sleeping, not necessarily in that order."

"That sounds good. You will need to rest up for what we have lined up for you in January."

This was something that Tollivar knew nothing about. "More speeches?"

"Many more. We are reaching a point where we are going to need to appeal to some of our corporate colleagues to put some money into some of our projects. We need more computers for our high school students. We need more Smartboards for our elementary and middle school classrooms. And if I may make a suggestion, Mister Tollivar; I know your speeches on the important roles classroom teachers play in the school has gone over well with our local civic groups, but I was hoping we could make some slight revisions."

"Such as?"

"We have programs that need to be mentioned. We need to let the public know the work the school district has done to modernize our campuses, the computers, Smartboards, and other electronic equipment we have added.

"And we need to tell them about our leadership team and how we have improved the atmosphere in our school district by adapting the principles of corporate culture."

"That's what we are doing?"

An audience was beginning to grow around Abigail and Tollivar.

"That is exactly what we are doing," she said. "And you as our Teacher of the Year are just the person to spread the message about how successful our school system has been."

For one brief moment, Tollivar was tempted to tell Abigail Saucier what she could do with her successful school system. "I will go over my speeches and see what I can do," he said.

"Good. Now we will need to be taking you out of class quite a bit during the second semester."

"I've already missed 12 days."

"You are far more important to us as a salesman for the school district than you are as a classroom teacher," she said.

"But wouldn't you think the Teacher of the Year should actually be doing some teaching?"

Abigail had clearly grown tired of the conversation. "I'll get back with you at the beginning of the semester," she said, "and I will e-mail your schedule to you by the end of the week."

Tollivar thanked her and then she moved on to another group of teachers.

Leron Hundley waited until Abigail had moved on before he approached Tollivar. "I've seen the type, Walt."

"What type?"

"You saw the damned movie. She's going to get you and your little dog, too."

It did not take long for the party to break up. Shortly after Abigail Saucier left, groups of teachers left Rollo's Pizza Emporium, shoveling the leftover pizza into doggy bags and quickly downing their drinks.

Abigail Saucier's appearance sent the message that their horrific fall semester was going to be followed by an even worse spring semester.

***

Abigail checked her cell phone- two voice mail messages, both from her mother, and text messages from her secretary and Diandra. Her daughter was not planning to be home until late, something that was happening with greater frequency of late. Abigail did not know what to do with the rebellious teen. Her daughter knew about her relationship with Bernard Feinberg and who knew what else she knew or suspected. Her mother wanted to know if she was coming over for dinner Friday evening. She started to call her mother, and then thought better of it.

She drove home and was not surprised to see that not a light was on in the place. Diandra wasn't there and neither was her husband. He rarely stayed at home any more, and she found that it really did not make any difference to her whether he was home or not. It had been a long time since the two had shared a bed and it had been longer since she had enjoyed being with him.

She looked down the block at the elaborate holiday decorations on nearly every house on the block- every house except the one in which she was standing.

There had been a time when the Saucier family decorated for Christmas. One year, she recalled, so many lights had been strung across the yard along with a recreation of the manger scene that the house had received first place in the annual Chamber of Commerce Christmas Lighting Contest.

She stepped into the garage, turned on the light, and saw the area where the old decorations had been stored. "Should I?" she said, looking longingly at the symbols of Christmas past. Maybe she could even get her family to help her put the decorations up.

She turned and flipped the light switch off. "What family?" she asked aloud. "What Christmas?"

She opened her cell phone and tapped the voice memo icon. "Thoughts for what we should do to bring up SAP scores at the high school and middle school levels."

Christmas would have to wait.

CHAPTER SIXTEEN

It did not take long for the word of Abigail Saucier's latest plan for bringing up SAP scores to spread. She had called a meeting of all principals during the Christmas break and told them the steps they would need to take once the second semester began to ensure that grades would increase on the standardized tests.

At the elementary levels, all classes except those mandated by the state would be totally eliminated to place complete emphasis on math and reading, the two areas covered by the SAP tests and by the federal No Child Left Behind program.

Students would be taking an average three hours of math and three hours of reading per day.

At the middle school and high school levels, extra emphasis would be placed on drills to improve test-taking skills. During home room, teachers would go over proper methods to answer constructed response questions, formerly known as essay questions, using tips offered through the new Guide to Passing the SAP Test manual that the Franklin Heights Unified School District purchased from Brockton-McGill.

All history and government classes would concentrate solely on reading and taking constructed response tests over the reading material. The teachers in elective classes, including music, home economics, and physical education would drop the regular curriculum, replacing it with even more reading and constructed response questions.

When the teachers questioned the changes, Principal Willis Shantz silenced them with the one word that had come to symbolize the school year. "We just have to buckle down and do it," he said. "We reached this plan by consensus, you know," he said at a faculty meeting.

Leron Hundley was not having any of it. "Damn, Willis. How the hell will we be able to play dodge ball if we're doing constructed response tests?'

"I am sure you will figure out something, but you won't have to worry about it tomorrow."

"We get to play dodge ball?"

Shantz shook his head. "You're going to the admin office for an LPI seminar."

"LPI. I don't want to take no damned LPI seminar. Send somebody else."

"No can do. We're sending you and five other teachers."

Tollivar spoke. "We can bend and twist our curriculum and make everything about picking up a point or two here and there on the SAP, but we're shortchanging these kids. They are going to leave this high school knowing nothing but how to pass a standardized test, and for that matter, just one type of standardized test."

"We reached this…"

"I know, I know, through consensus."

Shantz nodded. "Walt, I also have a message from Dr. Saucier. They want you and me to have lunch with some business leaders tomorrow. The superintendent is trying to convince businesses to adopt a school and bring a more business, results-oriented attitude to our buildings."

"But I've already been out three days in the past couple of weeks. I know, I know. If I do my job and prepare lesson plans, any trained substitute can bring what I bring to a classroom."

"That's why you're Teacher of the Year, Walt," Leron said.

The meeting continued with the instructional coach outlining plans for two evening sessions in which the school district would buy meals for any parents and students who wanted to come after school.

"Considering the number of students we have who receive free and reduced lunches, that is a great idea," Kayla said. "And it gives us a chance to bond with the community."

"Finally," Leron said. "Something that can help these kids and doesn't have a damned thing to do with SCRUTINY or SAP or constructed response."

The coach continued explaining how the evening socials would work.

"After we have our meals, some of our teachers will meet with the parents and let them know what they can do to help our students prepare for the SAP tests."

Leron leaped to his feet. "Say what?"

The instructional coach ignored him. "While those teachers work with the parents, the rest of the faculty will lead the students, both high school and younger siblings who may attend, in SAP-related activities."

"You'd have to be a SAP to come for something like that," Leron said.

"Nonsense, in addition to the free meal, the math portion of our evening will be a Las Vegas Night, complete with sizable cash prizes."

"Can't we get substitute teachers for this?" one teacher said.

The Three Amigos were muttering in the back of the room, noting that things like this had never been done in the past.

Not seeming to notice that dissension was brewing, the instructional coach resumed her presentation. "Now we need a catchy name for the evening."

"How about Hell Night?" Leron shouted.

"Or 'Are You Smarter than a SAP Tester?'" Michael O'Leary asked sarcastically.

"I love it," the instructional coach said. "That's what we'll call it."

"But I was joking," O'Leary said. It did not matter. The event had a name.

"One more thing," the instructional coach said. "Mr. Shantz has told me I can select three teachers to get out of classes for two mornings next week to plan this event. Of course, the district will pay for substitute teachers."

CHAPTER SEVENTEEN

It was the first of the week. Lucas Brock reached into his billfold and found only six dollars. He fished another 27 cents out of his pants pockets.

Six dollars and 27 cents. It would not be enough to satisfy that monster, he thought. Lucas stood outside the east entrance to Franklin Heights High School, shivering as a cutting wind accompanied a light mist. The doors were open; he could go inside, but those were not the instructions he had received from Rico Salazar.

After waiting nearly 10 minutes, Lucas saw Salazar and his two confederates, Rock and Chris, approaching him. He involuntarily flinched. How long was this nightmare going to continue?

Each Monday morning since the beginning of the school year, Lucas and others who were subject to taunting from other students paid $25 protection money to Salazar. That price prevented the Franklin Heights bullies from messing with him, but did nothing to stop Rico and those who followed him. They continued to verbally harass Lucas and the others, often accompanying their insults with a reduced, but still potent, physical harassment. Sometimes it was only at the level of "playful" shoving and punching. Other times, it was close to beatings. Through all of the pain he was suffering, Lucas knew one thing for certain- if he stopped paying the protection money, the beatings would be much worse.

And now he was $18.73 short and seconds away from being a punching bag for Salazar and his crew.

"If it isn't Little Lucas," Salazar said, greeting Lucas with a name he had hated from the beginning. "Does Little Lucas have a present for me?"

Lucas placed his right hand forward, holding a five-dollar bill, a one-dollar bill, a quarter and two pennies.

Salazar took the money, glanced at it, and then looked back up, a cold look in his eyes, a look Lucas had come to fear.

"This is six dollars and 27 cents."

Lucas nodded.

"Six dollars and 27 cents. I did not ask for six dollars and 27 cents. Where is the rest of my money?"

Lucas tried to answer, but no words came out of his mouth.

Salazar backhanded the frail youngster, who stood only a few inches over five feet, sending him to the sidewalk face down. Lucas felt the blood pouring out of his nose, as he tried to lift himself off the ground.

The effort was futile. As he started to rise, Rock put his foot in the boy's chest. He struggled, but he could not move.

"Do you know what we do with people who do not pay their money on time?" Salazar asked. Without waiting for a response, he looked at Rock and said, "You know what to do."

As much as he tried to steel himself for the impact, the first kick in his side sent Lucas into a state of shock. He whimpered quietly as the beating continued, seemingly for hours, but actually only for a few minutes.

"Can't anybody stop this?" the young man thought. As the beating neared its conclusion, he indulged in the only thought that brought him any pleasure during his nightmarish high school years.

Lucas envisioned his own finger, pulling the trigger of a gun and blowing away Rico Salazar and everyone else who had caused him pain.

It was a thought that crossed his mind more and more often with the passing of each day.

Rico Salazar was going to pay. Everyone was going to pay.

***

Are You Smarter than a SAP Tester was everything Tollivar imagined it would be and less.

After a spaghetti red dinner in the cafeteria, parents were taken to the auditorium, while the meager three dozen students who attended were taken into classrooms for activities centered on the test –taking skills they would need to ace the annual standardized exam.

After the parents were seated, the Franklin Heights instructional coach greeted them. "When it comes to success at our high school," she said, "you are the ones who make it possible.

In two short months, we will be taking the State Assessment Program or SAP as we call it. The results of those tests are critical to our students and to our school.

"You may be asking yourself, 'What can I do to help our students and our school succeed on the SAP test?'"

Not one person was thinking that, Tollivar knew as he surveyed the parents, most of whom came from poor families and were only here for the hot meal, the dessert, and the prizes.

The instructional coach continued, "You can help us by keeping your children on task, by letting them know how important these tests are and making sure that they do their best on the SAP tests, for the sake of our school…and of course, for themselves."

Tollivar knew and he figured most of the parents knew that the SAP results would not have the slightest impact on the children. If the scores were high, it wouldn't matter, because the bar would continue to be raised year after year in such a way that the school could never succeed.

If the scores went down, it was never the initiatives started by upper administration that were at fault, but the teachers, who somehow had failed to properly implement those initiatives.

"You can help your children succeed by giving them constructed response questions at home," the instructional coach said.

That suggestion caught Tollivar off guard.

"If you want your son or daughter to clean up his or her room, instead of just saying, 'Clean up your room,' you can ask the child to explain to you the results of not following your instructions. For example, you can say, "Why should you clean up your room?' And then when that question is answered, and please make sure your child restates the question, you can ask your child to tell you three things that could happen if the room is not cleaned, based on examples you have given them in the past.

"The ability to answer constructed response questions is vital to your child's success."

Despite the stirring ode to constructed response questions, Tollivar noticed a few parents were headed toward the exit.

The instructional coach knew exactly what words to use to stop them and the words had nothing whatsoever to do with constructed response.

"We will have a drawing for the door prize in 15 minutes. You have to be present to win."

Almost reluctantly, the fleeing parents returned to their seats.

In order to earn their prizes, they would have to answer some sample SAP questions.

They were trapped in a hell of the school's making, Tollivar thought, but at least they were smarter than a SAP tester.

CHAPTER EIGHTEEN

FEBRUARY

The first 16 girls entered the second floor bathroom, did what they had to do, gossiped about boys and discussed the pros and cons of various and sundry sexual positions, and even had one near fight. It was just a typical day.

Even the crude "Out of Order" sign on the third stall didn't put a dent in the traffic or slow things down…until the clear red pool of blood seeped out from under the stall and onto the tile floor outside.

A sophomore opened the door and discovered the lifeless body of one of the school's regular substitute teachers, Dorenda Plumb. At one time, Mrs. Plumb had been an English teacher at Franklin Heights High, but after taking maternity leave with her third child, she decided not to go back into the classroom on a full-time basis. Since that time, she had been at the top of the list when substitutes were called.

During the current school year, with teachers gone to one meeting after another, and others just calling in sick to get out of going to one meeting after another, she had been subbing nearly every day.

Abigail Saucier and Stanley Kramer were in a meeting in Carlton Dunn's office when he received word of the death.

"They're sure she is dead?" Dunn asked. He nodded as he received a response. "I suppose suicide has been ruled out?" Dunn paused. "I suppose suicide has been ruled out?" He continued nodding. "Thirty stab wounds, you say?"

A few moments later, when the call ended, Dunn breathed in deeply and then exhaled. "This is not a good day for a murder," he said. "We have the TV stations and the Daily News coming to the high school so we can announce our new initiative for the homeless."

"I don't think you have to worry about the reporters showing up," Kramer said.

"I suppose not. I'll need to call her husband and give him our condolences."

"What will we tell him?" Kramer asked.

"What can we tell him?" Abigail responded. "He just lost his wife and their three kids have just lost their mother."

"It will be tough to spin this in a positive way," Dunn said, staring out the window.

"Do the police have any suspects?" Abigail asked.

"Not yet. It has to be a janitor."

"Why do you say that?"

"We can't afford to lose any more students if we are going to improve our graduation rate."

"Maybe we will be lucky and she was killed by an underclassman," Kramer said.

"I hadn't thought of that. That would be just as good as a janitor." It was the first time Dunn had smiled during the conversation.

He began pacing the floor, wearing a path between his desk and the door. "We will have the press conference just as planned, but we will delay the announcement of the homeless initiative." As Dunn passed his desk, he punched the button on the intercom. "Celia, put the following message on the district Facebook page. Are you ready?" Dunn continued pacing as he dictated the message. "We are all saddened by the loss of Dorenda Plummer..."

"Plumb," Abigail corrected.

"We are all saddened by the loss of Dorenda Plumb, a longtime employee of the Franklin Heights Unified School District. Our staff will offer the police department our full cooperation in investigating Mrs. Plummer's death."

"Mrs. Plumb's," Abigail corrected.

"If this is determined to be a murder...

"She was stabbed more than 30 times!"

"If this is determined to be a murder, it will be the first time in the 89-year history of the Franklin Heights Unified School District that a substitute teacher has been killed on our watch. We are proud of the incredible protection that we provide to the teachers and staff. When substitutes come to our school, they know the odds are heavily against them being murdered. Let me see that before you post it, Celia."

Dunn looked at the assistant superintendents. "That is the way we are going to deal with this murder."

"You don't think she was killed by that Salazar thug, do you?" Kramer asked.

Dunn shook his head. "No, he's a partner in our graduation initiative. He knows that murdering substitute teachers is bad for business."

The mention of Rico Salazar brought an immediate involuntary physical response from Abigail. She still could not get her daughter's boyfriend out of her mind.

"Abby, are you all right?" Dunn asked.

"Fine," she said, as she snapped out of her daydream. Somehow, she thought, she had to get Salazar out of her system.

***

Despite the murder of Dorenda Plumb, it was business as usual at Franklin Heights High that day. The brutal stabbing did not cause half as much difficulty as the yellow crime scene tape that put the second floor girls bathroom out of business. Since one of the first floor bathrooms was already out of order due to vandalism, the remaining bathrooms were nowhere near enough to handle the traffic.

In-service meetings for the English Department went on as planned in the first floor conference room. Substitute teachers were hired to fill in for the English teachers to give them ample time to pore over results from the most recent SCRUTINY tests.

Dorenda Plumb had been scheduled to substitute for Kayla. As the teachers awaited the arrival of Abigail Saucier, who was going to conduct the meeting, the talk was about the reaction of the secretary who handled calling substitute teachers.

"She was pissed about having to call in a second sub," one teacher said. "She said she had already hired one substitute, it wasn't her responsibility to hire another and the district doesn't pay her enough for what she does."

"So did she get another sub?" Kayla asked.

The other teacher nodded. "She did, but not before she said, "What happened to the days when substitute teachers took better care of themselves?"

"She said that?"

"Yeah, she was really pissed that Mrs. Plumb let somebody murder her."

"They just don't make substitute teachers like they used to," Tollivar said.

***

When Abigail arrived, she brought several boxes of glazed doughnuts, a peace offering that did not mollify the teachers, who would have much preferred to have been in their classrooms rather than digging into test results. Nevertheless, the doughnuts immediately began disappearing.

After the brief social time, Abigail said, "Let's get down to business. Our SCRUTINY scores are down."

"They were testing the kids on things we have not yet gone over in class," Tollivar said. "We knew there were going to be some problems"

"We have to deal with those problems immediately. We are less than three months away from the SAP tests, and we cannot afford to lose any opportunity to prepare our kids to do well on these tests."

Rita Summers, a veteran teacher who handled upper level writing classes, voiced what had become a major concern for the staff. "How do you expect us to have higher scores on the SAP when we are allowing all of these hoodlums to roam the halls, and I do mean roam the halls, they are never in class?"

"That's your problem, Mrs. Summers, and you will have to deal with it" After that brief exchange, the smile returned to Abigail's face, as did the sing-song quality to her voice.

"Rita, I understand your concerns, but you know as well as I do, these children come from home lives that we cannot even imagine. It is up to us to provide them with a stable, safe environment. And that is exactly what you wonderful teachers do day after day, year after year.

"But giving these children that stable, safe environment is just part of why we are here. We are also responsible for improving scores on the SAP. And to that end, we have a new weapon in our arsenal that should make things easier for us- The SAP Diagnosis Website."

Tollivar suppressed the urge to groan. He was certain this weapon was going to backfire on the faculty.

Abigail continued, "The website was created by a mathematics instructor in the Hyland Park School District. It crunches the numbers, not only for each school district, but also for each student in that school district. We can gather more information about how our students did on last year's SAP tests than we have ever been able to do before.

"By spending time going through these numbers, we can determine not only the total scores the students made on the tests, but also the types of questions they missed. For instance, we can learn if our students need more work on answering constructed response questions."

"And what will be able to do with all of this information?" Tollivar asked.

Abigail looked at him as if he were a fourth grader. "This information, Mr. Tollivar, will enable us to do more differentiation in instruction than we have ever been able to do before. We can find which student is deficient in any particular area and we can tailor our lesson plans to that one student. For the first time, thanks to this website, we will be able to devise lesson plans for each student in our classrooms. In order for our children to succeed, we must differentiate."

"But I have 160 students!" Rita Summers said.

Abigail smiled triumphantly, "And now you can have 160 lesson plans. Each student will receive the attention that he or she needs to be able to succeed in our school and on the SAP test."

"But when will we have the time to be able to write all of these lesson plans?" Mrs. Summers asked.

Tenth grade literature instructor Becky Rondell added, "And how can we teach 30 to 35 lesson plans each hour? When we deal directly with just one student, what's to cause the other students from going wild?"

"Especially considering some of the kids we have in our classes this year," Mrs. Summers said.

Abigail glared at them. "You are all professionals. I know you will be able to deal with it. As for the time it will take to delve into these statistics, we are going to block off three days on the calendar when we will hire substitute teachers for the entire English department so you can study the statistics and start writing the lesson plans."

Tollivar was not pleased with this announcement. "So you are saying that we are going to be taken away from our students for three more days. Does anyone understand the value of actually having a teacher in the classroom?"

"Of course we do, Mister Tollivar," Abigail responded. "We have the best teachers in the state…but we also have the best substitute teachers in the state and this is an appropriate time to use them.

"Now that we have that settled, let's see what else we can do to improve those nasty old SAP scores."

"I don't mean to be insensitive," Kayla said hesitatingly, "but how can we be sitting here discussing this just a few hours after Mrs. Plumb was murdered right here in this building?"

"The police are handling the situation, Miss Newman," Abigail said. "The school district will make sure all of our teachers are safe. Dr. Dunn is sending out a memo today."

And with that reassurance, Abigail returned to the matter at hand. "Can we all agree that it is important that we make every effort possible to reach every child possible?" No one challenged the statement.

"And we can all agree that differentiated instruction is the best means to reach that goal."

Again, no one offered any argument.

"Then we have consensus. We can move forward. We can accomplish great things when we listen to each other and work together."

***

It didn't take long for gossip to travel the halls of Franklin Heights High School, especially when the news began with the sound of raised, angry voices.

The voices belonged to investigators from the Franklin Heights Police Department after they discovered that all of the brand-new, state-of-the-art video surveillance equipment, installed at great expense to district tax-payers, had been disabled, some of it smashed beyond repair, some covered by heavy black masking tape, and one, directly by the science laboratories in which the digital images had been replaced by a never ending loop of hardcore porn.

One of the officers had loudly proclaimed, "it's not even good porn."

The disabling of the cameras did not surprise Tollivar when he heard the news. That had certainly been done early in the school year when the roving gangs of drug dealers who had free rein wanted to make sure their illegal activities were not recorded.

Since Dorenda Plumb had been stabbed to death shortly after school, the odds against no one seeing anything suspicious were astronomical, but the police were unable to uncover a single witness with any useful information.

The news spread quickly that the police had no idea who the murderer was. That only added to the atmosphere of fear that enveloped the school.

Superintendent Carlton Dunn did not help matters any when he resorted to what appeared to be intended as a comforting video message sent by e-mail to all staff, and also shown at a brief faculty meeting.

The baby-faced administrator stared awkwardly at the camera for several seconds before the message began, looking in a mirror and combing a stray strand of hair back into place.

"My dear colleagues. I want all of you to know that we are saddened and shocked by the death of Dorenda Plummer, someone who was dear to all of us, and we are doing everything we can to help the police find the person or persons who did this."

There was a long pause before the video continued.

"Hasn't anyone heard of editing? Tollivar mumbled.

"Pardon me, friends," Dunn continued. "I meant to say we were shocked by the death of Dorina Plumb, someone who was dear to all of us.

"When Mrs. Plumb was discovered our emergency response team was immediately called into action. Grief counselors will be available today from 8:30 to 4:30 in the second floor conference room."

"Right by the bathroom where she was found," Tollivar thought.

"Because we were only able to hire two grief counselors due to budget constraints you will have to make an appointment before classes begin. To be fair, appointment times will be determined through a random drawing.

"While we are cognizant of the pain and suffering you are going through due to the loss of our beloved Mrs. Plumblee, we must remember how vital it is to the success of our students that we keep them engaged in learning all day. Nothing can ease a troubled student's day more than the welcome safety net of an engaging lesson plan. That is a lesson I learned as a third grade teacher before I decided to go into administration.

"Keeping the students engaged is also a way to keep them in school. While we are engaging their minds, we must also reassure these young people that they are safe when they walk the hallways at Franklin Heights High School. When they walk across the stage in three months to receive their diplomas, these students will thank you for the efforts you have put forth on their behalf. And hopefully soon, the horrifying, pointless death of our friend and colleague, Debra Plummer, will be just a sad memory in an otherwise wonderful school year."

As he finished his message, the video continued. "Are we done?"

"Yes, we're done, Dr. Dunn."

"How did I sound?" At that point, the video ended.

After the Smartboard hookup was turned off, Acting Principal Willis Shantz said, "Be careful today. Don't forget we will be pulling our designated at-risk students out of math today to fill out level-of-engagement surveys."

***

Officer Ed Brown, one of two police officers investigating Dorenda Plumb's murder, had a surprised look on his face when he saw the leader of the group that was blocking off senior hall.

"Rico Salazar! What the hell are you doing here?"

"Ed, my old friend," Salazar said. "Don't you know that education pays?"

"What can you tell me about the substitute teacher who was killed?"

"She wasn't that good of a teacher."

"She probably wasn't a good fuck either," one of Rico's friends added.

"Show some respect, punk!"

Salazar held out his arm as the "punk" started to go after Officer Brown. "Davey, settle down." Davey reluctantly stepped back.

"We don't know anything about the murder," Salazar said. "We don't want any corpses around here. It's bad for business if you know what I mean."

After a few more questions, Brown was rejoined by his partner, who had been working the junior hallway, and they headed toward the principal's office.

After they left, Diandra approached Salazar. As she reached him, she stood on tiptoes and kissed him, grinding her body against him as the kiss lasted for several long seconds.

As their lips parted, Salazar said, "Nice way to start a morning."

"I missed you last night."

"You know how business is."

"Can I come over tonight?"

"Let me get back to you."

A pouty look came over the teenager's face. "You know you're not that special, Rico Salazar. If I decided to find someone else, I would have boys lining up to see me."

"Diandra, those boys wouldn't be lining up just to see you, not with that body."

She smiled.

The smile disappeared when Salazar added, "But you can do whatever you want."

"I want to stay with you, Rico. Please let me come over tonight."

"I'll let you know after school."

"All right," she said. "I've got to get to class."

As she left, Rico felt his cell phone vibrate. He did not recognize the number displayed on caller ID. "It's Rico."

"Mister Salazar, this is Abigail Saucier."

"And what can Rico do for you, boss lady?"

"What do I have to do to get you to stay away from my daughter?"

A smile crept across the drug dealer's face. "How far would you be willing to go to protect Diandra from big, bad Rico?"

"I will do whatever it takes."

"Then we may just be able to do business. Can you meet me at my place at 6 p.m.?"

"Yes."

***

The school day seemed to last forever and none of Kayla's lesson plans worked out as she had hoped. She was one of the teachers who signed up for grief counseling, not because of any love for Dorenda Plumb- she hardly knew the woman, but because the stress of everything that was happening in the school year, from the physical attacks to the presence of known felons in her classroom was getting to her. During a small portion of the day, she felt a strange sense of security when Rock was in her room. He had protected her once and she knew he would do so again if there were ever a need.

The counseling never took place, however, since Kayla was not one of those fortunate few who won the grief lottery.

She was almost scared to death to leave her classroom after she graded some late papers from the end of school until shortly after 5 p.m., the time police estimated that Dorenda Plumb had been murdered.

Kayla straightened her papers, wrote out a handful of post-it notes for the next day, turned out the lights, and started to walk out the door. Before she entered the hallway, she opened her purse and felt a little safer than she had in quite some time.

She took out a small, black steel object, one she had told herself she would never go near. When a girl teaches at Franklin Heights High School, her best friend is her gun.

***

It was after Abigail Saucier screamed, "Oh My God," for the fifth time that Rico laughed and said, "Woman, how long has it been since you've had a good fuck?"

Fuck was a coarse, vulgar word, one that had rarely crossed Abigail's lips in her four decades, but she was quickly falling in love with it.

"Just shut up and fuck me!" she said, and he did, not once, not twice, but three times in the space of a couple of hours. When the sex was completed, Abigail crawled as close to Salazar as she could and rested her head on his chest, running her fingers through his thicket of black chest hair.

"Man," Salazar said, "I can see where Diandra gets it. And I can see that you haven't been getting it, unless Mama Finger and Papa Dildo have been giving it to you."

Now that the three hours of unbridled passion had ended, Abigail was beginning to think about what she had just done. She was a 40-year-old woman, not only sleeping with an 18-year-old boy, albeit one who had stopped being a boy a long time ago, but an 18-year-old boy who was her daughter's boyfriend. But maybe some good could come out of it.

"You will break up with Diandra."

"I'll think about it. She was disappointed when I told her she couldn't come over tonight. She's usually good for three times, too, maybe four, and she always leaves me with a blowjob."

"You're a pig."

Salazar took her hand and put it between his legs.

"You can leave any time."

Abigail said nothing, choosing to squeeze the fleshy object in her hands. "I do need to go," she said reluctantly.

"I'm not stopping you."

She climbed out of the bed and started putting on her clothes. Salazar remained naked.

After she finished dressing, Abigail headed toward the door, with Salazar a few steps behind her. They stepped into the hallway.

"How about a little goodbye kiss?"

Abigail leaned forward and brought her lips to his. After a rough kiss and a couple of long follow-ups, Salazar said, "Not bad, but that wasn't the kind of kiss I was talking about." He put his hand on top of Abigail's head, and she quickly fell to her knees.

Though it was not an act Abigail particularly relished, for some reason she was taking a perverse pleasure in pleasing the arrogant cocksure Salazar.

There was a slight noise at the other end of the hallway, but Abigail ignored it. The only thing that mattered to her at that moment was pleasing the boy in front of her.

When the act was finished, Abigail noticed that Salazar's eyes were trained on something at the end of the hallway.

With traces of Salazar dribbling from her lips, Abigail caught a brief glimpse of Diandra.

Salazar laughed. "You won't have to worry about her any more, Boss Lady."

"This will never happen again," she said. "It can't happen."

She bolted down the hallway, as Salazar called after her. "It will happen, Boss Lady. You can count on that."

As Abigail left, she failed to notice Diandra hiding around the corner.

"My own mother," the teenager said, examining her smart phone photo of Rico and Abigail kissing.

CHAPTER NINETEEN

The fistfight in the back of Kayla's room was not the first of the school year, nor the second, third, or even fourth. On the first few, she had called the office and had Officer Karl sent to her room. Now, she simply waited for the fight to end. There were never any consequences and the paperwork was a nightmare.

This time as the battle continued in her fifth hour class, one of the combatants pushed the other into a back row seat, knocking the seat and its occupant to the floor.

As the fighters moved to another area of the room, Kayla helped Lucas Brock get to his feet and started picking up his books.

As she reached for the final item on the floor, a sketchpad, Lucas tried to grab it away from her, but he was a split second late. It only took a second for Kayla to realize why he was so concerned.

"Lucas, what is this?"

"It's none of your business," he said, with a defiance Kayla had never previously seen. "That's my personal property."

The fight was breaking up as Kayla moved to the intercom and buzzed the office.

A loud noise, along the nature of a slightly muted air horn filled the room, signifying the office had received the call. "Stand by," a freakish, mechanized voice said.

Moments later, the greeting was followed by a human voice. "Yes, Miss Newman?"

"We need Officer Karl in my room immediately."

"Another fight?" the woman responded with a sigh.

"Please just send him into my room."

"Give me my notebook," Lucas said, reaching for the item in Kayla's hand.

She jerked her arm away. "No, Lucas. Please have a seat."

As he reluctantly moved toward the back row, Kayla examined the writings on the pad. It was filled with drawings of death and destruction, which was not that unusual for teenagers, but in this case, the drawings were vivid recreations of Franklin Heights High School settings, and some of the bodies, many of which are decapitated, that Lucas had drawn, were labeled with the names of students, with one, Rico Salazar, underlined three times for emphasis, and featuring a smiling gunman standing over him.

She leafed through the other pages in the pad and saw diagrams of the school. Her heart began pounding. Could Lucas Brock be another Klebold or Harris? Had she accidentally managed to find out about a Columbine-style massacre plot?

Sweat was pouring down Lucas' brow as Officer Karl entered. "Another fight?" he said, as he examined the furniture that had been knocked over during the scuffle.

Without saying a word, Kayla handed Officer Karl the pad. "Who's responsible for this?" he asked.

Kayla motioned for Lucas to join them. "Young man, you are coming with me," Karl said, taking him by the arm and escorting him out of the room.

Kayla breathed a sigh of relief. What would have happened if she had not discovered the threat, she wondered.

***

Officer Karl stayed with Brock as they waited for Principal Willis Shantz to finish a phone call to the central administration office.

After what seemed an eternity, but was only a few minutes, the door opened and Shantz waved for Karl to bring Lucas into his office.

"What do we have here?"

Karl handed Shantz the pad. "Some extremely disturbing stuff on this pad, sir."

Shantz examined the pad, peering over his glasses. "I'd like to see someone do that to Salazar," he said, quickly correcting himself. "Not that I think this is right, son. What do you have to say for yourself?"

"It was just a joke. I get bored sitting in Miss Newman's class and this is what I do to stay awake."

"Son, you do understand we have to call the police, don't you?"

Lucas started to plead, then simply nodded.

As Shantz reached for his phone, he spotted a memo by his desk. "Do not do anything that might end up in the news without consulting the admin office." He started to dial the police number, then noticed another memo and thought better of it. "We must keep our seniors in the class-room. The reputation of our school district depends on the number of people we have receiving diplomas." Shantz stood, crossed to a filing cabinet in the back corner of the room, opened a drawer and leafed through the files until he reached the one he wanted.

"As far as I can tell," he said, again examining it by peering over his glasses, "you have never been in any kind of trouble."

"No, sir."

"I would hate to see a perfect record ruined for something like this. However, there have to be consequences for this kind of thing. It would be irresponsible of me not to do something about these issues that you appear to have."

"Yes, sir."

"I am going to make an appointment for you with the counselor."

"Yes, sir."

Shantz sat behind his desk, pushed a button on his phone. "Please have the counselor come into my office," he said.

A few moments later, it was determined that the counselor's schedule was filled up for the next two weeks due to her role in analyzing SCRUTI-NY test data. "I can work him in for 10 or 15 minutes the first week of March."

"Fine. Now please, Mr. Brock. No more of this nonsense. You are only a few months from graduation. You wouldn't want to do anything to jeop-ardize that."

"No, sir. Can I have my pad back?"

Shantz shook his head. "Don't push your luck, young man. We will be keeping this. We do not take threats of violence lightly."

***

Five minutes later, the door opened to Kayla's classroom and Lucas Brock walked in, moved quietly to his seat and sat down as if nothing had happened. As Kayla did her best to continue with the lesson, she noticed him opening another notebook and start to draw.

As she always did, she worked her way around the room, eventually moving behind Lucas' desk. He had already drawn another scene of carnage, with one major difference between the new drawing and the one that was in the principal's office.

This one featured a decapitated teacher who clearly was meant to be Kayla Newman.

CHAPTER TWENTY

I can't deal with union complaints today," Carton Dunn said as he straightened his tie. "I have four radio interviews, I have to tape a spot for tomorrow's 'Wake Up to Franklin Heights' show, and we are shooting a YouTube public service message on how cool it is to graduate."

"No doubt about it, Dr. Dunn, you certainly are busy," Assistant Superintendent Donald Duckett said, "but these problems have to be dealt with. The union is not going to go away."

"Fill me in while I get ready," Dunn said, spraying his hair until each one was perfectly in place.

"Do you mind if I ask you a question, Dr. Dunn?"

"Shoot."

"If you're doing the radio programs this morning, why are you spending so much time on your appearance?"

Dunn glared at his assistant. "I am the superintendent," he said, as if that were the answer to all questions. When he noticed the puzzled look was still on Duckett's face, Dunn continued, "Whenever I am out in the public, whether it be on a television program, a PTA meeting, or like this morning, on radio, I am representing the Franklin Heights Unified School District. If I don't look my best, the school district looks bad."

"That certainly explains it, sir."

"Now what is the union up to this time?"

"It's about the murder of the substitute teacher."

"Why are they complaining? It was a sub. We have never had a full-time certified employee murdered in this school district, and it will never happen under my watch."

"We are having a difficult time finding anyone willing to substitute at the high school."

"No problem. We will just cut out all leave for teachers."

"What if they get sick or have to go to a funeral?"

Dunn pondered the question. "We can have teachers watch their classes during their plan periods."

"That's a violation of our union contract."

"Then double up on classes."

"Beg pardon?"

"If a teacher is gone, combine his class with another teacher's class, then education can go on without any problems."

"But they will be teaching different subjects."

"Education is education. We have hired the best teachers for our classrooms and they know how to roll with the punches," Dunn said.

"But we could have 60 students in a classroom!"

"I'm not saying it would be easy, but when times are tough, it's a time for the tough."

"Beg pardon?"

Dunn sighed. "Do I have to handle every little problem for this school district? Tell Abby to handle it."

"I like that idea, sir."

"Now what was the union upset about?"

"Pretty much everything I said."

"Abby will take care of it."

Dunn examined himself in the mirror.

"You look great for radio, sir," Duckett said.

***

The focus for the February STAR meeting was the upcoming SAP tests. In less than two months, Franklin Heights' students, as well as students across the state, would be taking the annual exams.

"During today's meeting," Abigail said, "we have to come to a consensus about what we can do to help our children successfully cross the finish line and increase our SAP scores. But first, before we start our productive day of helping our children succeed, let's do a team builder."

"I knew it. I knew it," Leroy said, in a voice audible to most of those gathered into the banquet room at the Franklin Heights YMCA, "we're going to do another damned team builder.

"Well, you can take these team builders and stick them right up your bony...

"Leroy!" Willis Shantz said.

"Well, she's not going to stick them up my bony Leroy," Michael O'Leary said.

Abigail glared at those at the offending table. When she was certain there would be no more outbursts, she continued. "Sometimes we forget that we cannot achieve anything if we do not communicate with our children, As a mother, that is something I think about all of the time.

"It has been many years since we have been in elementary, middle, or high school, and in those years we have lost sight of what is hip."

"Saying 'hip' ain't hip," Leroy said, drawing a "shh" from those at his table.

"While most of us grew up listening to rock or country, today children listen to an entirely different type of music- hip-hop or rap."

"That white bitch is going to show us how to rap?" Leroy said, making a move for the door, before he was grabbed by two of his fellow Franklin Heights High STAR team members.

"So today" Abigail continued, "we are going to have a rap session." She paused and pulled out a large roll of white tape. "Or should I say a wrap session."

"Oh, good God!" Tollivar said.

"Let's number off from one to 12. After you have said your number go to the section of the room that is marked with that number and wait for further instructions."

Tollivar was a "nine," while Kayla Newman, who was sitting beside him, was in the "10 group."

After all of the teachers and administrators were grouped, Abigail spoke. "One person in each group will be designated the mummy, while the others in the group, using the roll of tape and other materials which you have been provided, will make that person into a mummy and decorate him or her accordingly. When you are finished, we will vote on which team has the best mummy."

"Your mummy must have been one hard-assed bitch," a voice, which sounded unmistakably like Leroy's said from the middle of group four.

"What does this have to do with education?" Tollivar asked.

Speaking in her best elementary teacher tone, Abigail patiently explained, "When we work as a team, we not only cover everything the students need to know, but we do so in such a way that they will know the value of teamwork and what incredible goals can be accomplished when we all work together.

"Now choose your mummy and may the best team win."

***

"You're the Teacher of the Year. You have to be the mummy," a female middle school teacher said to Tollivar.

"Oh, no. Please let someone else have the honor."

The rest of the group, much to Tollivar's chagrin, quickly endorsed the middle school teacher's request.

"Sandy," Kayla Newman called from group 10, "trade me."

The woman replied, "I'm not sure Dr. Saucier would like that."

"Trust me. There won't be any problems."

When the swap had been completed, Kayla said, "I will be the mummy."

"We've already picked Mr. Tollivar. He's the Teacher of the Year."

"I will be the mummy," Kayla repeated, leaving no doubt she meant what she said.

Tollivar put his hand over hers. "Kayla, you don't have to do this."

"I will be the mummy," she said, quietly but firmly.

"All right. You're the mummy," one of the team said, and the wrap session began.

Tollivar mouthed a silent thank you to his colleague, and as the other teachers, most of the group consisting of elementary instructors, wrapped Kayla with the white tape, Tollivar stood to the side.

After 10 minutes, the wrapping halted and the contest began, with Leron Hundley's team winning with what he described as "the best damned mummy I've ever seen."

***

"Everyone return to your seats," Abigail said, glancing at her watch to make sure the meeting was still running on time.

"At each table, there are colored markers and butcher paper. At your table, I want you to discuss the things that you can do in your school to make sure that our children succeed when we take the SAP tests in April.

You will have three minutes."

As the conversations began, creating a low buzz across the room, Abigail felt her phone vibrate and took it out. "Mom, I am in the middle of a meeting."

"And you consider that to be more important than your own mother?"

"No, Mom. Of course, I don't."

"It won't be long before I'm not around any more. I'll bet you can't wait for that day to arrive."

"No, Mom. I love you, but I am in the middle of a meeting."

"Your brother's not like that. He always has time for me."

Of course, he does, Abigail thought. He hasn't had a job in almost three years. The rest of the conversation consisted of Abigail's mother talking and Abigail just saying, "yes, mom" or "no, mom." Abigail glanced at her watch. The table discussions were scheduled to end in 17 seconds.

"Mom, I have to go, I love you." As she started to put her phone away, she saw a text message from Rico Salazar. "Meet me tonight, babe, eight o'clock."

Abigail blushed. Why am I acting like this, she thought. If anyone finds out, I not only will lose my job, but I will never work in the education field again.

At the worst, she thought, she could wind up in prison. For an educator to have sex with a student was a felony. But then she remembered how it had been the last time she had been in the teenager's arms, the last time she had been beneath him, on top of him, to the side of him.

"What am I thinking," she said out loud, causing heads to turn at the nearby tables. Abigail looked at her watch again. Thirty-three seconds late.

Quickly regaining her composure, she said, "I thought I would give you some extra time since it is vitally important that we do whatever we can to make sure our children succeed."

CHAPTER TWENTY-ONE

MARCH

As Kayla graded writing assignments, she did not notice Tollivar enter the room. After they exchanged a few pleasantries, Tollivar asked, "How is the situation with Lucas Brock?"

"He doesn't say anything. Even when I address him directly, he refuses to talk."

"Can we get the counselor to talk with him?"

"She says she is too busy dealing with real problems."

"Real problems like compiling data from the SCRUTINY tests?"

Kayla nodded.

"What about Josh Mason?"

"He hasn't been a problem since Clinton started stopping by after every class period."

"Clinton?"

"Rock."

"You seem to have made a friend."

"You can never have enough friends when you are a teacher."

***

Only three members were on the roster of the Franklin Heights High School Outsiders Club. No one else even knew of its existence.

The first meeting was held in Lucas Brock's converted bedroom, a room that had initially been the basement. Lucas' mother was the only other person in the house, since his father, who had left the family years earlier, was serving 5 to 10 in state prison for dealing drugs.

Lucas' mother slept most of the day every day and lived off disability payments and other federal assistance. At the moment, she was between rehab stints, making her way steadily toward the next one.

The family also received support from Lucas' uncle, who had a successful restaurant upstate. He rarely visited, but his guilt checks were enough to keep the family in food and keep Lucas' mother supplied with either alcohol or the drug of the month.

The Outsiders Club was named after one of the few happy memories Lucas had of his schooling, a middle school teacher who had taught S. E. Hinton's teen classic, *The Outsiders*, to his class in seventh grade. The book, and the teacher, sparked an interest in reading that continued to grow over the next five years.

The other two members of the club were sophomores Benjie McCloud and Tanner Brigman, both of whom lived on the same block and had often been threatened and occasionally beaten by the same bullies, both on the streets and at school.

After the three entered the basement bedroom, Lucas locked the door.

"Why did you do that?" Benjie asked.

"Can't take any chances." Lucas flipped on the light, a bare bulb that descended from the ceiling, and then carefully pulled a chest out from under his bed, inserted a key and opened it.

The mouths of Lucas' two young followers fell open as they examined the contents of the chest.

"AK-47s!" Tanner said after a long pause.

Lucas nodded. "Four of them and plenty of ammunition to go around."

Benjie stared at his older friend. "Then we are going to do it." There was an unmistakable excited tone to his voice.

Tanner Brigman did not share that tone. "Are you sure this is a good idea?"

"We are going to do it," Lucas said, adding, "We have to do it."

"Lucas!" his mother's voice called out from behind the door.

He quickly closed the chest and slid it back under the bed. He did not have to worry about his mother discovering the chest and its contents since she did not have a key to the door and would never be inclined to do anything that smacked of housework.

"Yes, Mom."

"I'm going out for a while,"

"All right, Mom."

"Don't wait up for me. I may be out late with my friends," she said, which by now Lucas knew meant she planned to be in the bed of some man, any man, before the night was over.

"I won't wait up, Mom."

As she left, Benjie said, "That was close."

Lucas shook his head. "The one person we do not have to worry about is my mother."

Lucas pulled a much-used spiral notebook out of his backpack and opened it to a section about halfway through its pages. He signaled for his friends to gather around him.

"This is what we will do."

Tanner Brigman nodded. "Well, at least this should make school more interesting."

CHAPTER TWENTY-TWO

Abigail was growing more and more irritated with the tone and content of Walter Tollivar's speeches. It was easy for Carlton Dunn to like the positive attention Tollivar was bringing toward the school and for the teachers, because Tollivar always made it a point of mentioning the importance of students graduating from high school.

But his speeches were not limited to praise of teachers and the capabilities of students. In every presentation he made, no matter what civic group he was addressing, Tollivar, without mentioning any specific program or initiative, found a way to belittle her efforts to drag the school district into the 21st Century.

If Tollivar wasn't addressing the "culture of meetings," as he called it, he was criticizing the amount of times teachers were out of the classroom for what he referred to as "so-called professional development."

Tollivar was careful never to criticize the school or its administration. In his speeches, it always appeared as if these "evils," as he referred to them, were things that happened elsewhere and should never happen at Franklin Heights.

The Teacher of the Year totally ignored Abigail's efforts to convince him to promote the initiatives she had begun.

As she sat beside Carlton Dunn at a Kiwanis Club meeting, listening to Tollivar's stump speech, her fury grew.

"The teachers in the Franklin Heights Unified School District take their responsibilities seriously," Tollivar said. "We know that each day when your children step into our classrooms, you have entrusted us with their education, and thus, with their futures.

"Our job is to make sure that when they leave our classrooms, at the end of the school year, that they are fully prepared for the challenges that await them, whether it be at the next level of schooling, or in the outside world."

Abigail glanced at Dunn. The superintendent was eating it up. He leaned toward Abigail and whispered, "Best move you ever made, making this guy Teacher of the Year. He's dynamite."

"Yes, he is," Abigail said, gritting her teeth.

"The important thing for all of us to remember," Tollivar said, "is that when we hear the media continuing to rip us over and over, telling us that our schools are failing and that our teachers and our classrooms are inferior, they are not telling us the entire story.

"Over and over again, we hear the horror stories about the so-called evil teachers' unions, who are supposedly doing everything they can to keep bad teachers in the classroom. We hear about programs that can put college graduates into the classroom with six weeks of training and accomplish miracles that cannot be accomplished by veteran teachers who have had years of training, at the undergraduate and graduate levels and in the classroom.

We hear the nonsense about how we should all be judged by what our children do on poorly-written standardized tests."

"Here we go again," Abigail grumbled.

"What did you say?" Dunn whispered.

"Nothing."

"In some schools...and I know you might find this hard to believe," Tollivar continued, "they not only teach to the test, which does not ensure that our students will know anything when they graduate, but they take standardized tests to prepare for the standardized tests and..." Tollivar's voice slipped to barely above a whisper... "and they teach to the tests that prepare the students for the tests." The Kiwanis laughed while Abigail seethed.

"They not only teach to the test that prepares the students for the big stakes tests, but God help us, they give the students even more standardized tests to prepare for the practice standardized tests that prepare the students for the standardized tests."

He has to be about finished, Abigail thought, toying with the remnants of her dessert.

"That scenario is happening all over the United States...and it is happening in the Franklin Heights Unified School District."

Dunn, who was drinking his tea when the statement was made, almost did a spit take. He looked at Abigail. "How could he say something like that?" A few seconds later, he added, "Are we really doing that?"

Abigail did not answer the question. She was too angry. The Teacher of the Year had finally crossed the line and he was going to pay for it.

CHAPTER TWENTY-THREE

APRIL

Abigail Saucier's Marie Antoinette moment came the second week of April when she received word of massive faculty dissatisfaction with her educational initiatives.

"I can't believe this," she said, as she relayed to Stanley Kramer and Donald Duckett what she had learned from a friend on the high school faculty.

"With everything I have done to make Franklin Heights the number one school for educational collaboration in this country, how can they be dissatisfied?"

"That's just the way teachers are," Kramer said. "You give them meetings every day, pull them out of their classes for seminars so they don't have to mess with those pesky kids, and they still criticize you. You just can't please everyone.

"Abby, have you ever thought of taking a lighter grip on the reins? Not everyone moves at the same pace you do."

"We can't afford to rest, Stanley, our nation is falling behind in education and we have to do anything and everything we can to close that gap."

"Well, at the risk of offending you, Abby, couldn't we try something simple like leaving the teachers in the classroom and letting them teach?"

Abigail glared at him. "It's that kind of thinking that sets education back 200 years. No, we can't move backwards if we are going to succeed. We just have to bring the teachers around to our way of thinking."

"How are we going to do that?" Duckett asked.

"I have an idea."

***

The announcement that every Friday would be Casual Friday in the Franklin Heights Unified School District was greeted with little enthusiasm at the high school.

"Saucy must have heard the natives were restless and decided to give us what we wanted," Michael O'Leary said.

"If that bitch gave us what we wanted," Leron said, "we could just stick an apple in her mouth and start the spit turning."

"If that's where you want to stick the apple."

"Gentlemen," Principal Willis Shantz said, as he entered the teachers' lounge, "don't we have better things we can talk about?"

"We could talk about booting some drug dealers out of this building," Leron said.

Shantz left the room without responding.

Kayla entered, crossing to the refrigerator and placing her sack lunch, two tuna sandwiches and a banana, on the bottom shelf.

"Hey, Newman, are you all right?" O'Leary asked.

She nodded and quietly left the room.

As she passed by Tollivar's classroom, he waved. "Kayla," he called as he headed toward the door to greet her.

She kept walking.

"Kayla," he said again.

This time, she turned. "Good morning, Walt."

"Are you all right?"

"That seems to be the question today," she said, her shoulders slumping. After a few moments of silence, she spoke, "Everything is just starting to close in on me. I keep wondering if I can going to make it through the day and I wonder if I am really making a difference for any of these kids."

"You are making a difference, Kayla. I see that every day."

Tollivar put his arm around her shoulder and guided her down the hall. "Let's talk about it."

"I need to talk," she said, "but I am not sure I want to talk." She looked up at the veteran teacher and for one brief moment she thought he was going to kiss her.

And when he didn't, she was strangely disappointed.

"I'll be all right, Walt."

"Are you sure?'

She nodded. As they walked toward her class, another teacher stopped them. "Did you hear? We get to wear jeans every Friday."

"I hadn't heard."

Nor had she really heard that teacher. She had other, more important, things to think about.

CHAPTER TWENTY-FOUR

The first rumors about a planned shooting at Franklin Heights High School came on one of those ever so frequent days that Tollivar was absent from his classroom.

The Teacher of the Year was going through his Learning Practice Inventory (LPI) training.

Though it was getting harder and harder for the school district to find anyone to substitute after the murder of Dorenda Plumb, Todd Bender needed money and he wasn't going to let a little murder here and there stand in the way of achieving that goal.

Bender had been fired from his last three jobs, two of them for not showing up for work, the other one for showing up and quickly showing how incompetent he was.

He was an ideal substitute teacher.

He was also a popular one when, immediately after introducing himself to a disinterested class, he announced he was tossing the lesson plan and the students could do anything they wanted.

"Can I take a leak?" one student asked.

"Sure, as long as you don't do it in here," Bender said.

"Can I make out with my girl?" another student said, attempting to see just how far Bender's laissez faire attitude extended.

"If she lets you," Bender said, taking out his cell phone and surfing the net, oblivious to the raucous noise that surrounded him.

Bender particularly enjoyed viewing pornographic images of young girls on the web and it didn't bother him to glance at a few of the girls in the classroom and imagine them doing some of the things he was watching on the miniature screen.

"You've gotta love high school," he said.

Despite his preoccupation with the images on his phone, Bender did manage to overhear one conversation between two boys in the front of the room.

"When are they going to do it?" one asked.

"April 20. The same day as Columbine."

"They won't really do it. They're just posers."

"They've got the guns."

"I'm going to be gone that day."

"Me, too."

Bender abandoned his porn momentarily and checked his calendar. He wasn't scheduled to substitute April 20. No problem.

He closed out the calendar and seconds later, naked girls filled his screen.

***

"What we will be doing momentarily is only a drill," Principal Willis Shantz announced over the intercom. "We hold three of these lockdown drills each year so that we will be prepared if we ever have any kind of incident."

Students paid little attention as Shantz spoke. Any time an announcement was given was seen as an opportunity to talk. The students also saw any time an announcement was not being given as an opportunity to talk.

"Our drill will begin in one minute," Shantz said.

In his classroom, Tollivar said, "When they give the word, all of you need to go to the east side of the room."

"Which side is east?" one girl asked.

Tollivar pointed to the correct side.

"I thought that was west," she said.

"If you go where you thought was west and the rest of us go east, we should be in good shape," Tollivar said.

"So we're supposed to go east?" a boy asked.

"Head that way," Tollivar answered, pointing in the proper direction.

"The drill begins now," Shantz announced.

Tollivar pulled the door shut and watched as the students moved, much too slowly, to the east side of the classroom.

"We are supposed to remain quiet," he said, trying to be loud enough to get the students' attention, but not louder than he was supposed to be during an actual lockdown.

The students ignored his request.

The next noise all of them heard was a loud banging on the door.

"Let me in, let me in," a girl screamed.

Tollivar did not make a move. He was not going to fall into that trap again.

"Please, let me in!" the girl pleaded.

Again, Tollivar did nothing.

"Aren't you going to let her in?" a student asked. "What if there was a shooter? She would be dead."

"We are not supposed to let anyone in once the lockdown begins," Tollivar said. "If we do, we are taking a chance on endangering the rest of you."

The pleading stopped and the students waited another couple of minutes for Shantz to announce that the lockdown drill was over.

"That was a waste of time," one boy said. "We aren't ever going to have anything like that happen at Franklin Heights."

In the back of the room, Lucas Brock tapped his fingers against his desk, his expression betraying nothing.

***

It was the eve of the annual SAP testing and much of the Franklin Heights High School student body was seated on the rickety wooden gymnasium bleachers, waiting for the annual SAP pep rally to begin.

Since the assembly was held during the final hour of the day, many of the students, rather than going to the gymnasium when they were called down for the assembly, headed directly toward the exits, toward the parking lot, and toward sweet, sweet freedom.

Willis Shantz blew into the microphone twice, though he had been told countless times not to do so. It was the way he had tested whether a microphone was working for as long as he remembered. "Can you hear me?' he said. "Is this microphone working?"

Seconds later, a piercing sound emanated from the microphone.

"We can hear you already," a student in the back of the gymnasium shouted.

"Good afternoon, students. Tomorrow we take the SAP tests. Make sure you get to bed early and have a good breakfast so you will be prepared to do your best and make us proud of you."

Even with the microphone working perfectly, few people heard what Shantz said, and even fewer were making any effort to do so.

"It is my privilege to introduce to you the woman who is in charge of SAP testing in the Franklin Heights Unified School District, our assistant superintendent for curriculum, Dr. Abigail Saucier."

Maybe two people clapped their hands.

"Thank you," Abigail said, as she took the microphone. "Tomorrow is the most important day of the school year. Tomorrow is the day when we will find out how much you have learned. There are no students in this state who work as hard as our students and I know we are going to do well.

"Your scores have been improving on our SCRUTINY tests, thanks to your hard work. Tomorrow, all of your efforts will finally pay off."

"One more thing I would like to say before I turn the program back over to Mr. Shantz. When you leave the gymnasium, we have free ice cream bars, courtesy of the Franklin Heights PTA, in appreciation of all you have accomplished and in expectation of what you will accomplish tomorrow. I know that will make my daughter Diandra happy. She loves ice cream bars."

"She'll have to get hers later," a boy called out from the middle of the bleachers. "She left the school when we were called down for the assembly."

Another boy answered, "She's probably getting hers now. Rico's not here either."

Laughter spread across the gymnasium as Abigail's face reddened. Seconds later, she was saved by the cheerleaders.

"Give me an S!" the perky blond captain shouted, with a little less than half of the student body responding.

"Give me an A."

Less of the same.

""Give me a P. What does that spell?"

Abigail had already exited through a side door, heading toward a meeting in the high school conference room.

***

"What are these?" Tollivar asked, as he held an object that resembled a television remote.

"These," Abigail answered, "are the latest in technological developments by Brockton-McGill. We have purchased enough of these clickers for every student in the Franklin Heights Unified School District."

"How are they used?" Tollivar asked, adding, "And how much did they cost?"

Abigail ignored the second question. "The most important thing we, as educators, can do, is to make sure that all of our teaching is based on scientifically-proven data. To that end, these clickers will not only provide us with the data we need to best serve our children, but they will also give us immediate feedback on how the children are doing and enable us to differentiate our instruction so that no child is left behind."

Abigail began a power-point presentation. "As you can see, the S-10 clickers are designed to be used with SCRUTINY," she said.

As the next slide came into view, she continued, "We will incorporate the clickers into our lesson plans. The students will push the button corresponding to the answers they have chosen and we will immediately know how many students and which students have correctly answered the question.

"For those students who did not answer the question correctly, Brockton-McGill has provided study guides and miniature SCRUTINY tests that the students can self-administer."

"When will we begin doing this?" Kayla asked.

"I would like to run a pilot session immediately before and after our final SCRUTINY tests," Abigail said. "After that, we will begin using them next year. All of our teachers will be required to take 19 hours of training in how to use the devices."

"Nineteen hours of training to learn how to use a clicker?" Tollivar was not pleased with this development, though he was not surprised.

"It is not just a matter of learning how to use the clicker," Abigail said, explaining it to Tollivar and the other teachers as if they were students from her years in elementary classrooms. "We not only need to know how the S-10 clicker works, but we have to know how to modify our lesson plans so we can make full use of it."

"How has this worked in other schools?" Kayla asked.

"So far, we have no data. We are lucky enough to get these clickers under a pilot program being initiated by Brockton-McGill. Instead of using $78,000 of the taxpayers' money, which will be the amount the company will charge once the project is fully underway, we are only being charged $67,000."

"It's hard to pass up a bargain like that," Tollivar said. "You have to be careful how you spend the taxpayers' money."

"Exactly."

"But if everything has to be based on hard data, how can we take a flyer on something that has no data to prove that it works."

"Brockton-McGill has a long track record in education," Abigail said. "The state buys the SAP tests from them; we buy the SCRUTINY tests. These clickers are designed by Brockton-McGill to help school districts succeed on the tests. To have these devices and get an $11,000 discount- it's a win-win situation.

"And the best part of it is, "Abigail continued, "that instead of preparing one lesson to fit all students, with the use of the S-10 clickers and all of the data we will receive from them, we will be able to provide differentiated lesson plans for each student in the district."

"But when will we have time to prepare lessons for 180 to 200 students? Tollivar asked.

"We are professionals," Abigail said. "We will find the time. We will MAKE the time. Are all of us in favor of each student succeeding?"

The teachers either nodded or said they were.

"Excellent, then we have consensus. There is nothing more wonderful than when teachers can collaborate, share their feelings and opinions, and then do what is best for our children."

***

It was obvious to Kayla after surveying 24 of the 32 students she would have in her room for SAP testing that Willis Shantz' suggestion that the students get a good night's sleep had been completely ignored by most of them- at least the 24 who had bothered to show up.

Some students could barely keep their eyes open and others looked as if they had just climbed out of bed. Kayla handed out the test booklets and answer sheets and began instructing the students on how to fill in their names and then fill in the bubbles that corresponded to each of the letters.

As she had been instructed, Kayla told all students to make sure they identified themselves as Caucasian, African-American, Hispanic, Native American, or Asian. A few years earlier, a handful of students who were not at the top of the academic ladder could not figure out which one they were, marked "other" and then flunked the test, causing Franklin Heights High

School to fail to reach Adequate Yearly Progress in the "other" category on No Child Left Behind guidelines.

When the actual testing began, Kayla was not surprised that students continued to talk, in voices much louder than whispers, causing the students who actually wanted to succeed to have a hard time concentrating.

For a time, she tried to quiet the class, but her suggestion never took hold. Finally, she gave up.

As she walked around the class, she noticed students were answering essay questions with just two or three words, some were bubbling in the letter C on every multiple choice question. One student in the back was sleeping…and snoring.

And these were the students who were going to determine if Kayla was a success or a failure as a teacher?

***

"Mister Salazar. State rules require that you take your own test," Tollivar said, as his least favorite senior leaned back and relaxed, his feet propped up on the next desk while Chris bubbled in the answers on both Salazar's test and his own.

For a moment, Tollivar worried about what would happen if one of the state education officials who were on campus that day to monitor the administration of the tests (or SAP Police, as they were called) were to walk into his classroom.

And then he stopped worrying. It didn't matter. It just didn't matter.

***

Since most studies had shown that the best results on standardized tests are achieved during the morning hours, testing only lasted two hours on the first day. After that, cars began flying out of the parking lot. No one was going to try to track down truants on a SAP testing day. As long as they were there the next morning for the second round, no one much cared.

And there was no doubt the students would be back the following day. Thanks to the Tomorrow's Promise program started by Carlton Dunn, the school district's business partners were providing incentives to students, including prizes for drawings that were held at the conclusion of each of the testing periods.

The prizes included everything from televisions to computers to cash.

The business partners were also paying for many of the supplies regularly covered by the district budget, which enabled more money to be used for what was referred to as "strategic initiatives," especially anything that would improve the graduation rate.

Despite the prizes, the SCRUTINY tests and everything that had been done to lift test scores, Abigail had a sinking feeling that the bottom was going to fall out for Franklin Heights High School.

The SCRUTINY results indicated that scores would probably be flat for most of the students, with the possibility of them moving up or down a point or two. The problem was in the ones brought into the school through Carlton Dunn's graduation initiative. While a few of those rescued from the streets had buckled down and were working toward earning a degree, most of them were simply along for the ride.

That was why Abigail had dusted off her resume and was busily applying for any opening that would be a step up on the career ladder. The most attractive job opening, an assistant director position in the State Department of Education, was one that Abigail coveted. Not only would she receive a sizable salary increase, but also she would be able to remain in education, a field she dearly loved, without having to deal with the students who seemed to constantly get in the way.

As she watched Dunn examining himself in the mirror in preparation for another heartfelt message to district employees and patrons over the high school's cable television channel, Abigail applied postage to two more applications and dropped them into the outgoing mail slot.

"Do you think this tie makes my eyes stand out?"

"That was just what I was thinking," Abigail said.

That settled, Dunn applied the finishing touches and prepared himself for his latest fireside chat. "Are you ready, Craig?" he asked the photographer.

After getting a thumbs-up response, Dunn assumed a serious pose, sitting with what he believed to be his best side facing toward the camera.

The photographer pointed to him, the red light turned on and the message began.

"Good morning. Today was the first day of State Assessment Program testing for the Franklin Heights Unified School District. This is what we have been working toward all year long. Today and the next two days, we will find out what we have learned during this school year.

"When I came to this school district, I came with two goals in mind. The first one was to improve our abysmal graduation rate and we are well on our way to doing so. Teenagers who in the past would have been filling our welfare rolls and our prisons are now opening up windows of opportunity for themselves, thanks to what we have done over the past several months.

"But as proud as I am of our expected improvement in the number of students receiving diplomas this year, I am just as proud of the steps I have taken to make sure that our students are given every opportunity to compete with students all over this state and this nation on standardized tests such as the SAP tests we are taking this week."

Dunn had caught Abigail's interest. What was he going to say?

"Our implementation of SCRUTINY, an innovative testing program designed to improve our students' test scores, has revolutionized our curriculum and put this school district at the forefront of standards-based education. This was something I pushed for from the moment I arrived at Franklin Heights."

Abigail felt a tap on her shoulder and turned to face Stanley Kramer.

"The man's a visionary, isn't he?" Kramer said, smiling.

Abigail didn't answer.

Dunn continued, "With Learning Practices Inventory, we have made sure that our teachers are providing lessons that our students will find engaging. Our teachers no longer stand in front of the class and lecture all period or hand out work sheets and sit behind their desks grading papers."

"That ought to make the teachers happy," Kramer said. "When Dunn put in LPI, he made our teachers actually teach." He nudged Abigail. "The man's a genius, isn't he?"

It was difficult, but again Abigail said nothing.

"The list of our accomplishments is far too long for this brief message," Dunn said, "but we in the administration of the Franklin Heights Unified School District want you to know that everything we do is for the betterment of our children. They are our number one priority. Thank you for giving us the opportunity to work with these wonderful young people every day. It is truly a privilege and an honor."

With the camera off, Dunn asked, "How did it sound?"

"You did us proud, Carlton," Kramer said.

"What did you think, Abby?"

She bit her lip, and then said, "It brought a tear to my eye."

Dunn checked his watch. "Gotta go," he said, "I have a lunch meeting at the club. Keep up the good work."

So you can take credit for it, Abigail thought, but again, no words escaped her lips.

***

"You said you were going to show us how we could get the guns into the building without going through the metal detectors," Tanner Brigman said, as he walked with the other members of the Outsiders Club toward the high school.

"I still don't see how we can do it," Benjie McCloud said.

"It can be done." Lucas reached into his pocket and carefully took out a handgun."

"You can't bring that to school," Tanner said.

"Don't freak out. No one is going to catch me. Just watch and learn."

Lucas took his friends past the front door and headed toward the side.

"They won't let us go in through the teachers' entrance," Benji said.

"That's not where we're going."

The three went around the next corner. "This is it," Lucas said. "This is how we will get the guns into the school. The cooks open it every morning at six and it is never locked. They receive deliveries all day long."

"How do you know this?" Tanner asked.

"My aunt used to be a cook before she failed a drug test. There are no metal detectors and everyone knows me. They'll let me through and any-one who is with me. We're going to try it out this morning."

Lucas pulled the door open. No one paid any attention. As the three boys walked through, some of the cooks said hi to Lucas, the others just ignored them.

After they exited the kitchen, Tanner said, "Unbelievable. unfucking believable."

"Two days from now, that's how we will enter the building. They will never know what hit them."

***

Students in Kayla's second hour class were turning in their homework in baskets at the side of the room, when Diandra Saucier, busily talking with a friend, tripped over Lucas' foot and fell to the floor.

"You did that on purpose!" she shouted.

"I'm sorry," he said.

Before Diandra could respond, Salazar said, "You need to watch where you put your feet, Little Lucas. Apologize to the lady."

"I said I was sorry."

Salazar stood. "Apologize to the lady."

"Please sit down, boys," Kayla said, knowing that her words did not mean a thing to either of them.

"Apologize," Salazar said.

Lucas reached toward his pocket and for a brief second Kayla wondered if this was going to be what she had seen weeks earlier in Lucas' notebook.

Lucas pulled his hand away from the pocket and extended it to Diandra. "Let me help you."

"Don't touch me."

"Let me help you," Salazar said. For a brief moment, Kayla thought his offer was also going to be refused, but then Diandra took his hand.

Kayla continued staring at Lucas. Was there a gun in his pocket or was she blowing this way out of proportion? She looked toward her purse. Would she ever have the nerve to take out her gun and use it?

She hoped she would never have to make that decision.

***

Leaving nothing to chance, Abigail Saucier called a meeting of the district's principals immediately following school on the first day of SAP testing.

"Give me your assessment. How are we doing?"

There was no way any of the principals could tell her with any certainty if the students would succeed on the test. According to the strict guidelines set by the state, they were not even allowed to look at the books. Any temptation to cheat was eliminated.

"My teachers tell me that most of the kids looked like they were filling in the bubbles," a middle school principal said. "They couldn't tell me if they were filling them in with the correct answers."

"Did they seem confident?" Abigail asked.

"The kids?"

She nodded.

Unable to think of anything else to say, the principal answered, "We didn't have anyone cry."

"We did," an elementary principal said. "Three kids. I don't know if it had anything to do with the tests. One of them wet his pants."

"That always makes me cry," Willis Shantz said, receiving a frown from Abigail.

"What can we do tomorrow to boost our scores?"

"Convince some of our new students to go to another high school," Shantz said. "We have had several transfers from other schools during the past few weeks. Nearly all of them are on the lower end of the scale grade-wise."

"That happens every year," Abigail said.

"It's a shame we can't threaten them," Shantz said.

"Why not?" an elementary principal asked.

"It would backfire. Our teachers are terrified of the kids."

"Yes, they are, aren't they?" Abigail said. "And the kids are afraid of the same students who scare our teachers."

"What are you getting at?" Shantz asked.

"I may have a way to pull up our high school scores and those are the ones that have been worrying us the most."

"Care to share?"

Abigail shook her head. "No, I need to check on a few things and I will get back to you."

One thing Abigail knew for certain. Rico Salazar could get to students who were beyond the reach of the faculty.

And as much as she hated to admit it, she had been looking for an excuse to see him.

***

It was one of those civic functions that Carlton Dunn enjoyed so much and this one he had been eagerly anticipating. As the Elks Lodge members slowly moved through the serving line for their share of chicken, potato salad, and baked beans, Dunn worked the line. He made sure to ask about the mayor's wife and children and showed the proper concern for the fire chief who was scheduled to undergo surgery at the end of the week.

"Mr. Dunn," a woman called out, and from the way she said it, Dunn knew that he must know the woman from somewhere. He walked up to her and extended his hand. "It is great to see you. How is the family?"

"They're fine," the woman said, sounding strangely disappointed. Dunn moved on to the next person in line.

Dunn spotted Stanley Kramer and waved him over. When Kramer stood beside him, Dunn whispered, "Who is that woman?"

"That's Becky in accounting."

"In our accounting?"

Kramer nodded.

Dunn breathed a sigh of relief. "Had me scared for a minute. I thought I had forgotten someone important."

***

When the dinner concluded, the Elks Lodge president gave a report on the organization's activities, and then introduced guests, saving Carlton for last.

"And tonight's speaker needs no introduction," he said, and then proceeded to spend the next several minutes introducing him.

It didn't bother Dunn, who sat patiently as the president sang his praises.

Finally, the president said, "And without any further adieu, the superintendent of schools for the Franklin Heights Unified School District, Mr. Carlton Dunn."

After the applause died down, Dunn spoke, "I am humbled to be here tonight because you have entrusted me with your most valuable possessions, your children. And that is a trust I take seriously.

"So seriously that tonight I am here to introduce a new program that is specifically designed to make our schools safer for your children. I call it SAFE- our Students Are First Emergency plan.

With this plan, we are taking the first steps to make sure that we never have a Columbine at Franklin Heights."

CHAPTER TWENTY-FIVE

Abigail was on top of Rico, riding with wild abandon, when the door to his room opened and Chris came in with two bottles of beer. "Hey, man, sorry to interrupt," he said.

Abigail reached for the blanket, but Rico grabbed her hand. "Don't worry, Abby. He's seen naked women before."

"Please," she said.

"Why not?" Rico let go of her hand and reached for the beer his friend was offering. "Abby, you said you had something you wanted to talk over with me."

"Can't we get dressed?"

Chris laughed. "I've seen naked women before." After a few seconds, he added, "They're usually younger though. They're usually a lot younger. Not that you're bad for an older woman. For the most part, you're pretty smooth, a wrinkle here, a wrinkle there. You know, there is a a thing called plastic surgery."

Abigail looked pleadingly at Salazar.

"Better step out for a little bit, bro. Thanks for the beer."

Before he left, Chris said, "You're better looking than my grandmother. That's for sure. I saw her naked once and I couldn't eat for three days."

As the door slammed behind Chris, Rico asked, "What's the deal? You said you had something you wanted to me to do."

She reached for her blouse. "Can I?"

"Sure."

As she buttoned the blouse, she told Salazar her idea. "We have to make sure we do well on the SAP tests," she said.

"And what does that have to do with me?"

"If you tell them to do well, they'll do well."

Salazar laughed. "I don't know what kind of voodoo powers you think I have, Abby, but I can't make dumb kids smart by snapping my fingers."

"That's not what I'm asking you to do."

"Lay it out for me."

"It's not the stupid kids I'm worried about, it's the ones who don't give a damn, the ones who are going to shade in the bubbles as fast as they can and not even think about what they are answering."

Salazar nodded. "I get you. You want me to make sure they have some incentive to do well."

"Exactly."

"And what would be my incentive?" Abby started unbuttoning the buttons she had just buttoned.

"You have to do better than that."

"You haven't been complaining."

Salazar laughed. "The sex is great. You're a great fuck for an old lady." Abigail flinched as he spoke the words. "And I want you to keep coming back for more, at least when I don't have something else going. I just had something green in mind."

"How about $1,000?"

"You've got that kind of money to throw around?"

"Of course not, but the taxpayers of the Franklin Heights School District do."

Rico leaned forward and bit softly on Abigail's neck. "I'll make sure the taxpayers get their money's worth."

He rolled over and threw Abigail to the bed, ripping off her blouse and causing two buttons to fly across the bed.

"Damn it. I paid $200 for that."

As Salazar's hand reached between her legs, the blouse was forgotten.

***

5 a.m.

The digital clock by Lucas Brock's bed displayed the time as Lucas watched it, waiting for the time to magically change to 5:01.

It was still two hours before he would begin the daily walk to Franklin Heights High School...probably for the final time.

He couldn't wait.

***

The phone rang as Tollivar was brushing his teeth. He quickly rinsed his mouth and then answered. "Hello."

"Mr. Tollivar, this is Lucy at the administration office. Your clicker seminar has been canceled. It will be rescheduled at a later date. You will go to your regular duties."

"And those would be?" Tollivar was joking, but the woman took him seriously.

"At the high school, of course. You are a teacher."

"You're right. I don't know what got into me."

It was welcome news for Tollivar. The last thing he wanted to do was to attend an all-day seminar teaching him to how use something he did not think would be beneficial to his students. He needed to be in the classroom. Especially when they were taking the SAP tests.

Tollivar hated standardized tests and the farce they were making out of education, but since the results were so important to the school and to his students, being in the classroom was one way he could at least have a semblance of control over what happened.

It would be good to be back in class, he thought.

***

For a few brief moments, Kayla thought about calling in sick. Despite her exposure to every cold or virus the students brought into the school, Kayla had only missed two days in her two years of teaching. Finally, she put the thought out of her head.

It was back to SAP testing and another day at the office.

***

Diandra did not spend much time getting ready for school. After she easily sneaked out of her home the previous evening, she had stopped by Rico Salazar's apartment, only to hear the unmistakable sound of her mother's voice through the door as she was about to knock.

It didn't take her long to find a group of high schoolers partying at the quarry and after polishing off nearly two six packs by herself, Diandra accepted a ride home, crawled into bed without taking off her clothes, and despite a lingering odor, those were the clothes she planned to wear to school.

As she was about to head out the door, a thought occurred to her. There was one more thing she needed to be fully prepared for school. She returned to her bedroom, opened a drawer, reached under a pile of panties and bras, and took out her marijuana stash. Sometimes she just had to have a little pick-me-up to get her through the day.

***

Abigail checked her planner.

She had an 8 a.m. meeting in Carlton Dunn's office to discuss the new SAFE initiative, followed by a curriculum meeting at an elementary school at 9 and then a walk-through at the high school at 10 a.m. to see how SAP testing was progressing.

She glanced through her e-mail messages. Bad news right off the bat. Abigail thought she was going to have the rest of the morning without Dunn after the 8 a.m. meeting, but he let her know that he planned to be at the walk-through at the high school since there was going to be a newspaper reporter and a team from one of the television stations

"It's our duty to put our best foot forward whenever we have a chance to get our message to the community," Dunn had written.

***

Benjie McCloud and Tanner Brigman were waiting for Lucas at the corner of 17th and Maple. It was the same path they had followed to school every day for the past two years.

"Have you got everything?" Benjie asked.

Lucas nodded and reviewed the plan. When he finished, he asked, "Does everyone understand?

Tanner and Benjie nodded.

"At ten minutes past 11, when the bell rings for fourth hour, we meet at my locker."

A half hour later, using the cafeteria entrance, the three teens and their weapons were inside the school.

CHAPTER TWENTY-SIX

Day two of SAP testing began just like day one. Students arrived late at class, had to have number two pencils provided to them, since they never had any of their own, and by the time the preliminary activities were completed, the students were already 20 minutes behind.

Shortly after the first testing session began, Kayla noticed a student sleeping in the second row. She gently nudged him, but he did not respond.

"Jeremy," she said, speaking in a low tone to keep from distracting the other students.

"Jeremy," she repeated. Again no answer.

"Jeremy," she said, a little louder. This time, he stirred.

"What?" he shouted, stunning Kayla and causing the rest of the class to turn in his direction.

"You need to be working on your test," Kayla said, pointing to the paper in front of him.

"O.K." he said, and he followed that assertion by laying his head back on the table and immediately returning to his slumber.

"Jeremy," Kayla said.

He lifted his head and flipped her off. "Damn it, Miss Newman. Will you just leave me the fuck alone?"

"Go to the office, Jeremy."

He shook his head.

"Are you drunk?"

He nodded.

"Please go to the office," she said, wondering what she was going to do if he refused to take her up on her suggestion.

"Why should I go to the office?" he asked, slightly slurring his words.

Kayla spoke in a soft tone, hoping the other students did not hear her. "Because they have a cot in the office. You can catch up on your sleep."

"All right," he said, lifting himself up and leaving the room on wobbly legs.

Kayla breathed a sigh of relief.

Another disaster averted.

***

The SAP Police arrived shortly after 9 a.m.

They weren't really police, though they wore badges furnished by the State Department of Education. The job of the SAP Police was to make sure that no cheating took place during the high stakes tests.

Teachers had to read instructions aloud to the students exactly as they were written in the book, without veering even a syllable away. Once the test booklets were in the students' hands, teachers could do nothing to help any student with a problem.

Any poster or other item on the wall that could conceivably help a student even slightly had to be taken down or it could result in the school district being penalized.

The SAP Police team consisted of two women in their late 50s or early 60s, dressed in identical blue blazers with blue slacks. Both women had gray hair, glasses, and didn't appear to have cracked a smile since the millennium.

When the women walked into Leron Hundley's classroom, the coach muttered, "Oh, hell."

Not understanding exactly what he had said, one of the women responded, "Hello to you, too." Her voice was only slightly more pleasant than her demeanor.

Leron hoped the state officials would stay just a few minutes then move on to the next room, but for some reason, they did not appear to be in any hurry to go.

As the math test continued, the women walked around the back of the room, occasionally glancing at a booklet. Leron was prepared to plop back into his swivel chair when he saw Willis Shantz enter the room. With the principal present, that meant Leron had to begin walking up and down the aisles, looking as if he was diligently proctoring the test.

As Leron passed one student's desk, he saw Shantz exchanging a few words with the SAP Police then leaving the room. As Leron started to return to his swivel chair, he noticed one student finishing one page on the test and moving on to the next, only two pages were stuck together.

"Rapid Robert," Leron said, calling the young man by his nickname, "your pages are stuck."

Robert examined the pages. "Thanks, Coach"

"No problem."

But it was a problem for the SAP Police, who immediately began taking notes on their clipboards.

One of them motioned to Leron. When he reached the back of the room, she whispered, "I am serving notice on you, Mr. Hundley."

"Say what?"

"You have violated state rules."

"How the hell did I do that?" he said, his decibel level beginning to increase.

"Mr. Hundley, please keep quiet. The students are testing."

"I know the students are testing. How the hell did I break state rules?"

"You helped that student."

"His pages were stuck together."

"You know the rules, Mr. Hundley. Once the students begin taking the test, you are not allowed to help them in any way whatsoever. The young man would have noticed the mistake when he went back over the test to check his answers."

"These kids don't go back and check their answers, lady," Leron said.

"But that is in the instructions. We put that in there specifically so the students don't accidentally forget to answer one of the questions."

"When was the last time you were in a classroom, lady? These kids don't listen unless there is an IPod involved."

"Nonetheless, you shouldn't have told him about those pages."

"You can take those pages and stick them up your ass, lady."

"Sir, the students…"

"They don't have to look."

"I'm going to have to write you up," she whispered, as nearly all of the students had turned in their direction.

As her pen flew across the clipboard, Leron said, "And you can stick that referral in the same place."

As soon as they finished taking their notes the two women moved toward the door.

"And you can stick these SAP tests up your ass, too. That's about all they're good for."

The students had begun to talk, until Leroy took the whistle he wore around his neck and blew into it, piercing a few eardrums in the process.

"Get back to work. This testing is serious business."

***

For once, Rico Salazar was doing his own test. Tollivar had moved Chris to the front of the room. For a short time, Salazar amused himself by tossing a quarter in the air, then using the results to determine his answers, and then he started whistling. Following the tried and true rule that all teachers were taught during their first year, the rule of proximity, Tollivar moved in Salazar's direction and the whistling stopped.

As Tollivar started to move on, Salazar raised his hand.

"Yes?"

"Drink of water."

"Not now. Wait until we have finished this part of the test."

"I'm thirsty now."

"It won't be much longer." Tollivar moved away.

After a few moments, Salazar's hand was up again. Tollivar walked in his direction.

"Drink of water."

"When the test is over."

"Not good enough, man." Salazar stood and walked out of the room.

Tollivar made no move to stop him. It wouldn't have done any good, he thought. He glanced at the test booklet. Despite the coin flipping and other nonsense, from what Tollivar could see, Salazar was answering the questions correctly and doing all of the required work.

Sadly, he thought, the evidence from those pages backed up what Tollivar had thought all along- this drug-dealing former dropout was one of the smartest students at Franklin Heights High School.

***

As Salazar moved into the hallway, the students in Kayla's room had finished the first part of the math test and were allowed to get a drink or go to the bathroom.

Salazar spotted Diandra. "Hey, babe. We on for tonight?"

She shook her head. "You were with my mother last night."

"Just business, baby. She wanted some help with leaning on some people to get good scores on these tests. I told her I would help her."

"How did she pay you?"

"Good old American dollars, courtesy of the taxpayers. Don't you just love the free enterprise system? Now, come on, baby. You don't want to disappoint Rico, do you?" He smiled and that was enough for Diandra's resolve to weaken.

"I'll think about it."

"Is that the best you can do?"

"All right. I'll see you tonight."

He pulled her into his arms and gave her a quick kiss. "That will have to do you until tonight," he said.

Salazar turned and ran into Lucas Brock. "Watch where you're going, Little Lucas."

For a moment, it appeared Lucas was going to say something, but he kept silent. In a couple of hours, he would give Rico Salazar his response.

***

The students were nearly halfway through their English test when a student in the back of Kayla's class raised his hand. Without waiting for her to come back to him, the young man said loudly, "I've got to piss."

Kayla spoke in a calm, measured tone. "You can go when everyone is finished with the test."

"I can't wait," he responded. "I've got to piss now."

She again responded quietly, "You will have to wait until we are all done with the test."

"I'm just going to leave," the young man said and started to stand up, only to find himself unable to move, with Rock's hands holding down both shoulders.

"You're not going anywhere," Rock said.

"Clinton," Kayla said, then thought better of it and remained silent.

"I've got to piss," the young man said.

"You heard Miss Newman. You'll wait until we're done with the test."

The young man said nothing. The problem had been taken care of and was running down his pants leg.

***

For some reason, Lucas Brock was having no problem whatsoever with the SAP test. In the past, he had always struggled, but this time, for whatever reason, everything was coming to him easily.

Every few minutes, he glanced at the digital clock on the wall. The English test was almost over. After the test booklets were turned in, the students would be released to their fourth period classes.

At that point, things at Franklin Heights High School would never be the same.

CHAPTER TWENTY-SEVEN

Benjie McCloud was the first of the three conspirators to arrive at Lucas Brock's locker. His SAP test has been administered by a substitute teacher, who was absolutely thrilled at the opportunity to dismiss his class a couple of minutes early.

The sophomore's hands were shaking as he waited for Lucas and Tanner Brigman to arrive.

"What are you doing, young man?" Principal Willis Shantz said from behind, startling Benjie.

"Nothing, nothing," he said, wondering if the principal had somehow discovered what they were planning.

Shantz had not even paid attention to his answer and had already disappeared around the corner.

The bell rang, again startling Benjie. A few seconds later, Lucas Brock was standing beside him, followed quickly by Tanner Brigman.

"Do you know what to do?" Lucas asked.

"Yeah," Tanner said. Benjie nodded.

The three waited until it was almost time for the bell. Lucas worked the combination lock on his locker, slowly and deliberately.

"It's about bell time, boys," Leron Hundley said, as he walked past them toward his room.

The boys mumbled a response.

Though it was almost bell time, clusters of students were mingling in the center of the hallway, boyfriends and girlfriends squeezing in each last moment of precious time before class, other students simply trying to stay out of the classroom for as long as possible.

The bell rang and scurrying students ran into classroom doors as the final note was sounding. Soon the only people left in the hallway were Lucas, Benjie, Tanner, and a couple of stragglers.

Lucas completed the combination on his lock and the door swung open revealing the weapons he had smuggled in through the cafeteria that morning.

Lucas handed each of his friends a weapon. "I'm going to the upstairs hallway. When I get there, you know what to do."

Benjie nodded. Tanner had already begun moving toward the end of the hallway. Lucas slipped his gun under the long jacket he wore. Benjie did the same. For the first few years after Columbine, trench coats had been banned at Franklin Heights High School, but the prohibition had vanished as memories of Columbine dimmed.

Benjie and Tanner placed themselves at opposite ends of the downstairs hallway and waited for Lucas to get into position. When he was upstairs, he gave the OK sign, and Tanner moved toward the fire alarm.

Seconds later, the piercing sound of the alarm screeched through the school building and students began pouring out of the classrooms, some moving in the single file order that was specified in the manual, others darting out the door as fast as their legs would take them.

Officer Karl, who was making his rounds upstairs, was the first one to see a weapon. It was the last thing he ever saw as Lucas pulled the trigger and watched as the school's resource officer flew backward.

It wasn't that hard, Lucas thought. I can do this. And soon, students and teachers were scurrying to find a hiding place.

As the students entered the downstairs hallways, they found themselves caught in a crossfire between Tanner and Benjie with nowhere to go.

A few tried to go upstairs only to find Lucas waiting on them. As they tried to go back in their rooms, that presented another obstacle. During fire drills, the protocol specified that teachers shut off the lights and lock the doors as they leave the rooms.

Students shook the doors to no avail.

They had no way to protect themselves.

***

Kayla felt a bullet zip above her as she knelt with her key to try to unlock her door. As the door opened, Kayla fell to the floor with something heavy on top of her as students rushed around her nearly trampling her.

She panicked when she saw a stream of bright red blood covering the side of her blouse. She wondered if she was in a state of shock and would be feeling the pain shortly.

Then she saw Rock lying beside her, drenched in blood.

"Clinton!" she shouted.

No answer.

"Clinton!" She shook him and his eyes opened. "They didn't get you, did they, Miss Newman," he said.

"No, Clinton. I'm all right. Hang in there; I'll get you a doctor. She tore off her jacket and started to rip it to form a makeshift bandage for the student, but it was too late.

Rock had breathed his last.

Kayla started to cry then remembered the situation they were all in. She pulled the door shut even as bullets ripped through the classroom, miraculously not hitting any of the students.

"Get down," she shouted to the other students and for the first time all year they did exactly what she told them to do. "We're going to get through this."

Kayla crawled behind her desk, fumbled in her pocket for the keys to it. After she dropped them to the floor, she picked them up, inserted the key in the bottom drawer and opened it.

At first, she hesitated. Then she opened her purse and took out her gun. Initially, she had a difficult time holding it. It seemed to burn her hands and she wanted to drop it and never look at it again. Kayla took a deep breath and suddenly the weapon seemed cool to her touch.

When the students saw it, they backed away from her. She lifted the gun and aimed it at the door. If anyone entered the room, she was going to get off at least one good shot.

***

"We will be safe in here," Carlton Dunn told the administrators, secretaries, and media representatives who were in Principal Willis Shantz' office.

For the past half hour prior to the firing of the first bullets, they had been discussing Dunn's SAFE plan.

One of the television reporters commented, "This would be a good time for that SAFE plan of yours to start working."

Dunn remained silent.

Suddenly the sound of Lee Greenwood's "God Bless the U.S.A." filled the room. Abigail had neglected to put her cell phone on vibrate. "Mom, I don't have time now. I am all right. I don't know about Diandra. I am sure she's O. K. She has to be. I don't have time to talk now, Mom. Yes I will call you when I find out anything." When the call ended, Abigail said, "Where are the police? Why aren't they here yet?"

"They should be here any minute," Shantz said. "I called as soon as I heard the first shots."

"What about your resource officer?" Dunn asked.

"I haven't heard anything from Officer Karl," Shantz said. "He may not be in a position where he can call us."

The phones continued to ring off the hook as the beleaguered secretaries tried to keep up with the parents who had heard about the shootings on radio, television, or through cell phone calls from their children.

"Mr. Shantz. Mr. Shantz," the voice of Leron Hundley came through the principal's radio. "Do you read me?"

"What's the situation, Leron?"

"Three, maybe four shooters, and from the looks of things, they have enough ammo to hold out for a quite a while."

"Where are you at, Leron?"

"I am with six kids. We weren't able to get back into the classroom. We are in the downstairs boys bathroom."

"Do they know you're in there?"

"Not yet, but I'm expecting them any time."

"Be careful, Leron."

"I'm sure the hell not going to take any chances," he said. "I've got a state championship caliber team next year."

Over the radio, the administrators heard a loud banging sound.

"What is it, Leron?"

"Looks like my time's up," the coach said. "But if ol' Leron ain't gonna be around any more, I'm going to take one of those little bastards with me."

***

Getting out of the hallway and back into his classroom after the fake fire drill was easier for Tollivar than for the other teachers since he had absentmindedly neglected to lock his door on the way out.

Every few seconds, he involuntarily flinched as he heard the sound of gunfire in the hallway. The room was dark with only a ray or two of sunlight coming in through the narrow window in the corner.

Girls were crying in the back of the room, as were a couple of the boys. No one was talking, except for a group in a back corner that had been praying non-stop since they returned to the classroom.

And for Tollivar, the anxiety was beginning to build. It was the scenario he had dreaded his whole life. He was trapped in a small, enclosed place, surrounded by people. Adding the stress of multiple shooters on the loose and he was teetering on the edge of a panic attack.

"I can do this," he whispered quietly. "I have to do this."

He jumped as he felt a tap on his shoulder and turned to see four students surrounding him, led by Rico Salazar. For a few seconds, Tollivar was unable to breathe.

"Any plans to get us out of this?" Salazar asked.

Tollivar tried to push his phobia out of his mind. He could not let his students know that he might not be able to cope with the situation.

"I don't suppose you would have some kind of weapon with you?"

Salazar laughed. "What do you think I am, Tollivar, some kind of stereotypical drug dealer?"

"I was hoping."

"You do know that Diandra was out of the room when the class started."

"I know. Don't plan on doing anything heroic. The police will be here any time. They will take care of her."

"Heroics are the last thing on my mind, Tollivar."

As the conversation ended, Tollivar felt relief. As far as he could tell, the students had no idea their teacher was only a few short moments from losing control.

***

Abigail opened the laptop on Shantz' desk.

"What are you doing?" the principal asked.

"I need to know where Diandra is."

"You can't do anything."

Abigail didn't reply. She glanced at the schedule. Her daughter was in

Walter Tollivar's class.

The sounds of gunfire were coming closer. "We can go into the walk-in vault," the attendance secretary said. Shantz nodded and the secretaries quickly moved into the vault.

"Go ahead, Dr. Dunn," Shantz said. "I'll stay and wait for the police."

"Are you sure?" Dunn asked.

Shantz nodded. "Dr. Saucier, you need to get in there with them."

"I'm not going anywhere, my daughter is out there."

"You can't do her any good if you wind up with a bullet in you."

"I'm staying out here."

Shantz nodded to Dunn to get inside and then closed the vault door. He glanced out the window and said, "The police are here. Thank God!"

Within moments, heavily armed police officers were surrounding the high school and a command station was set up about 100 yards away from the front entrance. The phone rang on Shantz' desk. He had ordered the secretaries to stop answering it a few minutes earlier since there was nothing they could do to lessen the anxiety of parents who were wondering what was happening with their children.

Shantz took a chance that this would be the police, and it was. Within a few moments, he was telling the officer in charge everything he knew about the building. Though the police department had a copy of the building plans, there were always things about that a principal knew about a structure that could not be found on any blueprint.

As Shantz continued talking, the doorknob to the principal's office began turning.

"They're at my door," he said.

"We're coming in," the officer said. "Hang in there."

Two shots rang out and the door was open. Benjie McCloud aimed his weapon directly at Shantz and Abigail. "Time's up," he said and began a cackling sort of laughter.

Before he could do anything, the front door to the school burst open and a half-dozen police officers entered the building. Benjie turned. "Drop the weapon," an officer shouted.

IF Benjie had done so, he might have survived. When he raised his gun to fire, he was torn apart by the officers' fire and fell to the floor in a bloody heap.

Abigail headed out the door. "Lady," an officer said, "you can't go out there."

"I have to go," she said, not stopping. "I have to make sure my daughter is all right."

***

"All right. We've got one chance," Leron said. "Follow me." He slammed his fist through the window. "Go!" he shouted.

"But we might get hurt if we jump."

"You might get killed if you don't jump, you damned fool!"

The student jumped and five others quickly followed. The bathroom door burst open as Leron headed for the window. Tanner Brigman fired, hitting Leron's shoulder just as the coach jumped.

Leron hit the ground, rolled, and kept running until he was behind the police barriers. A paramedic rushed to him. "Let me look at that."

"It's just a scratch."

"It's a bullet wound. You can never be too careful with those."

As the paramedic worked on him, Leron shook his head and said, "Damn. They don't pay teachers enough."

***

After Leron Hundley and his students exited the bathroom, Tanner Brigman returned to the hallways. Though he had the guns and the ammunition, he worried about entering a room and being jumped by several students. He hadn't thought about it at the time, but he wished Lucas had worked on a better escape plan.

There was no way this was going to end well for him.

In a few minutes, he was either going to be dead or headed for jail for a long, long time.

Everything had happened so fast, he thought. Would anyone know that he was one of the shooters if he somehow managed to ditch his weapons?

Then he saw it. An open locker. Tanner pulled a handkerchief from his pocket and began wiping the fingerprints off his gun. He knew he only had a few seconds. He could hear the police as they stormed the building.

He placed the weapon in the open locker, and then slipped into the bathroom and began hitting his head against the concrete wall. The pain was overwhelming, but it had to be done.

As he heard the voices grow nearer, he dropped to the floor and closed his eyes.

Just in time.

The door opened. "Kid, are you all right?"

Tanner didn't answer.

The officer got on his radio. "We've got a student down in the first floor bathroom. It's not a gunshot wound."

Tanner heard the next message on the officer's radio. "We've found weapons in a locker on the first floor. It looks like we're down to one shooter."

Tanner opened his eyes.

"What's going on?" he asked.

"You're going to be O. K., kid," the officer said. "It looks like you may have a concussion. We'll get you to a doctor."

"What about the boys with the guns?"

"They aren't going to hurt you, kid. You've got nothing to worry about."

Diandra Saucier had been playing a game of cat and mouse with the shooters since the siege had begun. Her decision to celebrate the end of SAP testing with a joint had been ill advised. No sooner had she entered the second floor bathroom and lit up than the first shots had been fired. For a time, she remained in the bathroom, and then she slipped out and tried to stay out of sight as much as possible. That strategy almost backfired. Twice, bullets barely missed her, ricocheting off the lockers and criss-crossing the hallways.

When the shots appeared to be coming from the opposite end of the hall, she sprinted down the stairs, at least as fast as she could sprint in stiletto heels, and moved toward Mr. Tollivar's room. If she could get back into the room, she thought, Rico would make sure she stayed safe.

Diandra was only a few feet from her goal when Lucas Brock, whose back had been turned, swung around and looked her right in the eye.

"No," she said, "Please, please, don't shoot me."

Lucas aimed the weapon. Before he could pull the trigger, Diandra darted for the door to Tollivar's room. She started banging on it as Lucas squeezed the trigger. The bullet hit a few feet above her head.

Diandra banged on the door over and over. "Let me in. Let me in!" she screamed.

Lucas prepared for his second shot. He pulled the trigger and nothing happened. It was time to reload.

"Let me in, please. He's going to kill me," Diandra shouted.

Lucas' gun was reloaded. Abigail rounded the corner just as Lucas aimed the weapon for his second shot at her daughter.

***

The voice in his head was telling Tollivar to curl up in a ball and wait for everything to be over. He found himself shaking uncontrollably, but the banging on the door shocked him out of the panic attack.

He remembered the warnings he had been given when he botched the lockdown drill at the beginning of the school year. You never open the door during a lockdown. If you open the door, you are putting all of your students at risk. Leave the heroics to the police.

Tollivar could hear Abigail screaming for the shooter to not kill her daughter. "Screw them," Tollivar said, pushing his fears aside. He flung the door open, pulling in Diandra just as Lucas fired another errant shot. Diandra ran to Salazar and collapsed in his arms.

Lucas began firing one shot after another at the door keeping Tollivar from closing it. Lucas ran toward the door and caught it before it could be closed.

"Salazar, you've had this coming for a long time," he said. He fired and Salazar fell to the floor.

"You bastard," Lucas shouted. "You're going to die." As he started to move in for the kill, Tollivar grabbed his leg and pulled up on it, throwing Lucas to the ground. "Get out," Tollivar shouted, and students began storming into the hallways.

Lucas grabbed his gun, which had fallen a few feet from him and jumped to his feet. Meanwhile, the students from Kayla's class, taking advantage of the situation, were also heading into the halls and to safety.

Lucas ran into the hallway and started firing indiscriminately. It was too late for him. The students were already in the schoolyard.

The police were headed toward him. Lucas turned. The last thing he ever saw was the face of Kayla Newman. Three shots sounded, one after another, and Lucas Brock was dead.

Abigail ran into Tollivar's classroom. "Diandra!" she shouted.

"She's hit," Salazar said.

Paramedics were in the room moments later working to save Diandra.

"Is she going to make it?" Abigail asked.

Not stopping the work for a second, a paramedic answered. "She's lost a lot of blood, but we'll do everything we can for her."

Abigail had never made a practice of it, but now praying was the only thing she could do.

***

Five dead, including two of the shooters, and seven injured, the police captain told Carlton Dunn and Willis Shantz.

"What about the third shooter?" Shantz asked.

"No sign of him, but don't worry, we'll get him. It looks like he wiped his prints off his gun, but they'll be on the bullets. It's only a matter of time before we nail the kid."

"But until then, he's out there with the student body."

"I doubt if he'll try anything again. This didn't work out exactly like they planned."

"Thank God for that."

A reporter for the local TV station approached the superintendent. "Dr. Dunn, do you have the time for a statement?"

"I will make the time," he said. "It is vital that our parents and the community know everything we are doing to make sure our children remain safe."

Dunn spotted a mirror on a secretary's desk and quickly checked his hair.

"All right, Dr. Dunn. Please tell us what happened today."

"Sadly, four students and a member of our staff died today in what can only be described as another incident of senseless violence. This is something that has worried me for quite some time and something that we plan to address with our new SAFE initiative. Sadly, the plans that were drawn up by previous administrations were inadequate to deal with the troubled element we have in today's society."

Another camera was focused on the paramedics as they carried Diandra Saucier on a stretcher and loaded her into an ambulance, her mother following right behind them.

As the ambulance pulled away from the school, Abigail ran her fingers through her daughter's hair.

"If you can pull my baby through this, God," Abigail said, "things will be different." Diandra's eyes opened. Abigail smiled and held her daughter's hand.

***

One of the most difficult tasks for the police was to hold back the hundreds of parents who arrived at the school after word leaked out about the shooting.

Though some had heard on television, radio, or by word of mouth, most had been kept informed by their children contacting them by cell phone. Though cell phones were supposed to be kept in lockers, according to school rules, nearly everyone had phones with them every minute of every school day.

Parents were told that hundreds of students had been killed and that others were dying. When they arrived at the high school, they could not understand why they were not allowed to pick up their children, even after word reached them that the shooters were dead.

Finally, secretaries with enrollment lists allowed parents to take their children, making sure they signed them out first. School officials wanted to make sure that they kept track of every student.

Some parents wept as they took their children off the school grounds. Others shouted angrily at school officials that they would never allow their children to set foot in Franklin Heights High School again.

Kayla had not stopped shaking since she had taken Lucas Brock's life. She had dropped the gun to the floor immediately after firing the third shot. The second and third shots had not been necessary. It was the first one that ended Lucas' threat, but there was no way Kayla could know that for sure.

The police questioned her for more than a half hour. Though it was Lucas Brock and not Kayla who had been terrorizing the school, it was Kayla who had to produce a conceal-carry permit to prove to authorities that she was legally carrying her gun.

Despite the shaking, Kayla's voice never wavered through the questioning. It was only after the officer left that the tear gates opened.

Tollivar put his hand on her shoulder. Without saying a word, she fell into his arms, and he held her as she cried.

***

Tanner Brigman listened to the evening newscast and was pleased when he heard there were still no clues to the identity of the third shooter.

Police were awaiting the results of fingerprint tests, according to the reporter.

Those tests won't make any difference, Tanner thought. He had wiped all of his prints off the gun and Lucas had loaded the weapon. The authorities would probably suspect him at some point since he was known to be a friend of Lucas Brock and Benjie McCloud, but they would never be able to prove anything.

The phone began ringing. After it rang three times, Tanner realized his mother must have passed out again. That happened on a regular basis ever since his father had cut out two years earlier.

Tanner picked it up on the fifth ring.

"I know what you did, white boy."

"Who is this?"

"You know who it is. It is too late for Little Lucas and your other friend, and your time is coming. It may be tonight, it may be next week, or it may be next year, but someday soon you are going to be just as dead as your friends."

And then there was silence. Tanner slowly replaced the phone on the hook.

He was a dead man.

Rico Salazar would make sure of that.

Tanner picked up the phone again and dialed 9-1-1.

"My name is Tanner Brigman. I am the shooter you are looking for," he said.

As the conversation ended, Tanner waited for the police to arrive. He was not looking forward to prison, but who knows?

"When I get through," he thought, "I will be the most insane person Franklin Heights has ever seen."

Living in a mental hospital was not what he imagined for his life, but he would receive three meals a day and would never have to face Rico Salazar.

It was the lesser of two evils.

CHAPTER TWENTY-EIGHT

School was dismissed for the next two days to give officials time to plan on how to deal with the aftermath of the shooting. When school resumed, counselors from all of the buildings in the district were called to the high school to talk to any students or staff members who felt they needed help.

Attendance was down nearly 30 percent as many of the students did not feel comfortable returning and many had parents who were not sure they would allow their children to return.

The district had to scramble when four teachers called in absent and the regular substitutes refused to work. Murdered substitute teachers and school shooters did not make for a friendly work atmosphere.

Diandra Saucier's condition had been upgraded from critical to stable, though she was still being kept at the hospital. Confident her daughter was going to make it, Abigail returned to work. Among the e-mail messages she had to sort through that morning was an invitation to interview for a state department position. Because she had not looked at her mail in two days, she was only now discovering she had an interview that afternoon. An interview for the position of director of curriculum for the entire state. It was a job she was meant to have, a job where she would no longer have to deal with glory hogs like Carlton Dunn or lecherous old men like Bernard Feinberg.

Dunn called a meeting for the afternoon to push ahead with the SAFE program. "It's more important now than ever," he said, but Abigail said she could not attend.

"I have to stop by the hospital to see Diandra," she said, making the lie as convincing as she could. She was not going to miss the most important interview of her life to work on building Carlton Dunn's resume.

The buzzer sounded. "Dr. Saucier, Mr. Tollivar is here."

"Send him in."

Moments later, Tollivar entered.

"Have a seat, Mister Tollivar."

After he sat down, Abigail said, "I need to have your resignation turned in to me by 5 p.m. today."

Tollivar didn't speak.

"Do you understand what I am saying?"

He nodded.

"Why?"

'You broke the school rules when you opened the door to your room and endangered your students."

"If memory serves correctly, my decision to break the rules saved your daughter's life."

"That's the way you see it. My daughter is lying in a hospital bed. She nearly died because of you."

"Because of me?"

"That is what I want you to say in your resignation letter. Please make sure to send a copy to Dr. Dunn and another one to the Board of Education."

Tollivar stood. "I don't intend to send a letter to anyone and I intend to keep teaching in this school district."

"That's not the way this is going to play out, Mister Tollivar. The last day of this term will be your last day, as well."

Tollivar walked toward the door.

Abigail stood. "If that's the way you want it. Someone is going to have to go and if it is not you, it will be Kayla Newman."

Tollivar hesitated. "Why Kayla? What has she done to you?"

"Not a thing. You are the one I want gone. You have caused troubles for me all year. You have criticized everything I have tried to do in this school."

"You have nothing against Kayla. You can't fire her."

"Wrong. Unlike you, Miss Newman does not have tenure. She has no protection whatsoever. And after all, why would the Franklin Heights Unified School District want to keep a teacher who killed a student?"

"You have to be kidding. That student nearly murdered your daughter."

"I am not interested in arguing with you, Mister Tollivar. Have your resignation on my desk by 5 or say goodbye to your friend. And one more thing…"

Tollivar waited.

"No more speeches. Your reign as Teacher of the Year is over."

Finally, Abigail Saucier had said the one thing that could make Tollivar happy.

***

Abigail's interview for the State Department of Education position went smoothly. She was fully prepared for every question they asked her. She was given the time to explain the programs she had initiated at Franklin Heights, including the implementation of the SCRUTINY tests and Learning Practice Inventory. The six-person interviewing panel, four men and two women, appeared to be hanging on every word she said.

By the time the 45-minute question-and-answer session was over, Abigail felt she had an excellent chance to climb another step up the career ladder. She would no longer have to play second fiddle to empty suits like Carlton Dunn.

She shook hands with each of the interviewers and headed out the door. As she left, she stopped, reached into her purse and pulled out a tissue. She didn't really need one, but she was hoping to overhear something that might indicate what chance she had of being hired.

"Very impressive," she heard one of the women say.

There were murmurs of agreement.

One of the men said, "I'm surprised she didn't try to take credit for her school's efforts to improve the graduation program, too."

Abigail's heart sank. She wasn't going to get the job. She was going to be stuck in dead end public school administrative posts forever.

"Who am I going to have to screw to get a better job?" she sighed.

***

Some students never returned to Franklin Heights High School after the shooting spree, so it was a much smaller graduating class, which was scheduled to receive its diplomas during Sunday afternoon ceremonies in the football stadium.

A section had been reserved for parents of the graduates, another for "distinguished guests" from the school district's business partners, and the rest of the seating was first come, first served. As usual, the ceremony had the trappings of the modern day graduation in which solemnity and decorum had been replaced by raucous catcalls and the constant sounding of air horns.

The students, walking faster than they ever did to get from one class to another, nearly raced across the football field as the high school band played the traditional processional, "Pomp and Circumstance."

After the students were standing in front of the blue metal folding chairs in front of the bleachers, the student council president stepped out of the group and stood behind the lectern.

Defying the United States Supreme Court, she said, "If you will all bow your heads," and she proceeded to give a two-minute prayer for the graduating class, ending with "May God protect us all in whatever we should decide to do from this day on. In Jesus' name we pray, Amen."

Willard Shantz introduced the board of education and a few distinguished alumni, and then turned the microphone over to Carlton Dunn.

"Distinguished business partners, Mayor Charles, members of the Board of Education, parents, and most of all, our graduating seniors, I had planned to tell you I was standing before you for the final time as superintendent of the Franklin Heights Unified School District. When our fiscal year closes on June 30, I had planned on turning the duties over to someone else and beginning my new job with the State Department of Education."

Dunn's words were the first sign of hope for Abigail in a long time. Even if she was out of the running for the state department job, if Dunn was going to take it, she might get the Franklin Heights superintendent position.

"Though my time at Franklin Heights has been short, it has been richly rewarding. No further evidence of that is needed than the members of our graduating class who are sitting in front of me.

"When I came to this community, I promised that we would increase our graduation rate and that promise has been kept. Last year, only sixty-eight percent of the students who entered this school as freshmen received their diplomas. This year, that number is 84 percent.

"And that is why I have decided to stay at Franklin Heights. My work is not done. Next year, we will improve the graduation rate to 90 percent."

Dunn waited a few moments for applause, which finally came, starting as a trickle and developing into something resembling lukewarm.

As Dunn continued, extolling the virtues of the graduating class, Abigail seated in the second row onstage behind the distinguished business partners, slid her smart phone our of her purse and checked Google News, typing in "Carlton Dunn." She still had a few moments before she would go into the audience, wearing her lapel mike and make two surprise scholarship presentations.

As she glanced at the news headlines, it was apparent the news had just been released. Under the headline, "Franklin Heights superintendent turns down state position" As she scanned the article, she noticed a listing of Dunn's accomplishments At Franklin Heights:

-LPI: The article indicated Dunn had started Learning Practice Inventory.

-STAR: Steering Toward an Achievement Renaissance. The article said Dunn was responsible for starting the leadership group in the Franklin Heights School District.

The article said Dunn was responsible for adding the SCRUTINY tests at the school, and implementing technological advances, including clickers.

"When I came to Franklin Heights," Dunn was quoted as saying, "I had a vision of what this school could be and I threw my heart and soul into making that dream a reality."

Abigail turned off her smart phone, the drone of Dunn's address ringing in her ears.

Everything she had worked for would forevermore be credited to Carlton Dunn.

"I screwed that fat slug for nothing," she said to herself.

Dunn stopped talking and a murmur ran through the crowd, with sounds of shock, accompanied by laughter.

"Oh my God," she thought. "The lapel mike." Her face turned a bright crimson as all eyes turned in her direction.

Dunn resumed his speech. "Congratulations again to our graduating class, the highest percentage of graduates to ever cross the stage at Franklin Heights High School. And now, our assistant superintendent for curriculum. Mrs. Abby Saucier, will make a special presentation."

As Dunn turned, Abigail was nowhere in sight. She dashed away from the portable stage. Stanley Kramer quickly stepped to the lectern and announced, "Unfortunately, Dr. Saucier has been overtaken by a sudden illness." He made the presentation, replacing Abigail's idea of surprising the scholarship recipients in the audience by simply having them come to the stage.

Outside the stadium, Abigail ran to her car, which was parked in an area reserved for school officials and dignitaries. For the next 20 minutes, as the ceremony continued in the stadium, she sat in the front seat and cried.

"This can't be happening to me," she thought. "This can't be happening."

She felt her phone vibrate. "Mom, I don't have time now."

"Did you hear about Carlton Dunn?"

"Yes, Mom."

"You can't let him take credit for what you have done."

"There's nothing I can do about it, Mom."

"No daughter of mine would take something like this lying down," her mother said.

Abigail put down the phone.

"God help me," she thought. "I am going to end up just like her."

CHAPTER TWENTY-NINE

Darkness was descending on Franklin Heights as Tollivar cleaned out his desk for the final time. He placed the wooden plaque he received as Teacher of the Year at the top of his fifth plastic crate of materials.

At first, he thought about taking more. So many memories were in the two gray filing cabinets he had used for 15 years. A few papers did make it into the crates, but most of the papers found their way into the trashcan.

There wasn't enough room in Tollivar's apartment for everything he wanted to keep, but he had no desire to spend money on a storage unit that he would never visit.

One crate contained yearbooks for each of the years he had taught in the school district. Each year, including this year, he had allowed students to sign his yearbook and now those short, sometimes comical, sometimes poignant messages were all he had left of his years at Franklin Heights High.

Tollivar stacked the boxes outside his classroom, took one last look around, and then left the classroom. He glanced at the wooden Room 210 above the door. For a brief moment, he thought about taking it down. "No, that's vandalism," he thought, as he picked up the first two boxes and started to move toward the stairs. He tripped, and the top box tipped, and a screwdriver fell out.

Tollivar looked at the sky and said, "I will take that as a message from you." He placed the boxes on the floor, stood on one that was filled with books and began unscrewing the wooden "Room 210."

Three trips up and down the stairs and he was ready to leave the school. Across the hall, he noticed that the light was still on in Kayla's classroom.

For a brief moment, he thought about leaving without saying goodbye to her. Certainly he would see her sometime. Maybe she would be at the mall or perhaps she would be walking down a street or eating at some restaurant.

And perhaps there would never be another moment. For a time, they would communicate through e-mail, Facebook, maybe a phone call or two on birthdays. But it would never be the same.

And that more than anything, Tollivar realized, was what he was going to miss about Franklin Heights High School. As much as he loved the students, these past two years with Kayla Newman in the room next door had been the best years he had spent in education.

It was Kayla who made everything bearable- the unruly students, the faculty meetings, the unspeakable administrators and their ridiculous priorities.

Tollivar put his final crate on the floor and headed for Kayla's room.

He knocked, but then entered without waiting for a response.

"Everything packed?" she asked.

Tollivar nodded. "Last crate is in the hallway."

"I can't believe you're not going to be here this fall. You're the reason I became a teacher."

She stood and walked over to him and threw her arms around him. "I don't want to let you go." After a pause, she added, "I thought about quitting."

"You can't do that. You were born to be a teacher. I have never seen anyone who was as ready to step into a classroom as you were."

"Sometimes I wonder if I'm just fooling myself."

"We all wonder that. I have never had a day where there was not at least one time when I wondered if it wasn't time for me to find some other line of work."

"What are you going to do?

"I have a line on a new job."

"At another school?"

Tollivar shook his head. "No, I'm going to take a break from the classroom. It will do me some good, and it will probably do the kids some good, too."

"I'm going to miss you." A tear ran down her cheek.

For one brief second, Tollivar thought about kissing her, but the second passed.

He pulled away from her, and then turned around and pulled her slight frame to him, giving her the kiss he had been dreaming about for the past two years.

At first, after their lips parted, there was an awkward silence, which was finally broken by Kayla.

"It certainly took you long enough."

He didn't wait any time at all for the second kiss.

"Do you have any plans for dinner?'

"No, unless you're asking me."

"I'm asking." Maybe there was something to be said for unemployment.

CHAPTER THIRTY

SEPTEMBER

As the new school year opened at Franklin Heights, the staff still was forced to endure another pep rally. "Why are we still doing this?" Donald Duckett asked Stanley Kramer.

"It makes Abby happy," Kramer replied. "The last school year was a tough one for her."

***

For Kayla Newman, like many other teachers, three months away from students had given her enough time to recharge her batteries and strengthened her commitment to her profession. She couldn't wait to see high school students pouring into her classroom for the fall semester.

"Hey, Newman, how's it shaking?" Kayla looked at Leron Hundley.

It was good to see him, she thought. He sidled up next to her and said, "When do you think we'll do the first damned team builder?'

Kayla laughed. It was good to be back.

***

It was the first major attempt by a newcomer to encroach on Rico Salazar's territory since he was 14. The self-styled "Mad Dog" McCready never knew what hit him.

Two of his men were shot, one stabbed, though none of the wounds were life-threatening, and the fearsome "Mad Dog" lay bleeding on the sidewalk, the hell beat out of him by three members of Rico's gang.

When the battle was over, Chris looked at Rico and said, "Man, they got you," as blood soaked through his leader's shirt.

"Don't sweat it, man. The fucker just nicked me."

As the police sirens blared in the background, Rico's men deftly slipped into their waiting cars and left the remnants of Mad Dog's crew.

As their car sped off, Chris said, "That felt good, man."

Rico nodded.

After a long silence, Chris said, "School's starting. Do we have someone lined up to deal?"

Rico shook his head vigorously. "No way, man. I'm sticking to the streets. High school is too fucking dangerous for me."

***

"What is it?" Abigail said as she answered the call from her daughter.

"I'm not coming home tonight.

"You are most definitely coming home, Diandra."

"I'm spending the night with Suzy."

"And I suppose Suzy's mother will back you up?"

"She will unless she's on meth again."

"You're not staying at Suzy's house."

"See you later, Mom. Love you."

Abigail smiled. Her relationship with Diandra had not improved.

She replaced the phone and knocked on the door to Carlton Dunn's office.

"Come on in, Abby."

She still hated the name, but she could live with it. Abigail locked the door behind her. Dunn patted his lap and in a few seconds, Abigail was seated squarely in the middle of it.

"We don't have much time," Dunn said.

"It won't take long," she said, a resigned tone in her voice as she began unbuttoning Dunn's shirt. Carlton Dunn was no great lover, by any stretch of the imagination, but he was much better in bed than Bernard Feinberg.

And sometimes, she thought, as Dunn began a ham-handed exploration of her breasts, a girl has to do what a girl has to do.

"I love older women," Dunn said as he buried his face between her breasts.

"Someday, I am going to kill him," Abigail thought.

***

During a rare lull at his new job, Tollivar completed his paperwork and thought about how much his life had changed over the past few months.

He no longer had to stay up until past midnight grading papers and constructing lesson plans. He still had meetings to attend, but nothing like the constant onslaught he had to suffer during his time in the Franklin Heights Unified School District.

Tollivar had the security of knowing he could return to Franklin Heights for the next year. He could have returned in September. Abigail Saucier may have been ungrateful for him rescuing her daughter, but Diandra was not. Once Diandra had texted him photos of Abigail and Rico Salazar kissing, Tollivar confronted Abigail, who had immediately tried to convince him the firing had been a big mistake. She told him he could return to his classroom immediately.

That, however, was not what Tollivar wanted. His demands were simple. He would return to work the following school year and no action of any kind would be taken against Kayla.

In another year, Tollivar thought, maybe he would be ready to return to education and once again bask in the overwhelming pressure of standardized tests, tests to prepare for standardized tests, and tests to prepare for the tests to prepare for standardized tests.

Until then, he could enjoy his growing relationship with Kayla Newman and serve as a sounding board for her when she dealt with the problems he was escaping for a year.

Tollivar felt a vibration and took his smart phone out of his pants pockets. He smiled as he read Kayla's simple three-word text message- "I love you!"

Within seconds, his response was headed toward his former and future colleague.

The opening of the door to his workplace interrupted Tollivar's musings. He put down his paperwork, straightened his blue blazer, put on his best workplace smile, and said the words the former Teacher of the Year would repeat hundreds of times that day.

"Welcome to the Franklin Heights Wal-Mart."

RANDY TURNER

Randy Turner has been an English teacher in Missouri public schools for the past 14 years. Prior to entering the teaching field, Turner was a newspaper reporter and editor for two decades. He has authored or co-authored six non-fiction books, including *5:41: Stories from the Joplin Tornado*, *Spirit of Hope: The Year After the Joplin Tornado*, *Scars from the Tornado*, *Newspaper Days* and *The Turner Report* and three novels, *Small Town News*, *Devil's Messenger*, and *No Child Left Alive*.

DON'T MISS THESE OTHER BOOKS

DEVIL'S MESSENGER
by Randy Turner

SMALL TOWN NEWS
by Randy Turner

Made in the USA
Charleston, SC
24 June 2013